*For Barry, Tom and Gemma
and for my mum*

Born in Gower, South Wales, Karen Lowe moved to Shropshire when she was five. After a BA degree in French, German and English Literature from the University of London, she worked as a secretary in Fleet Street and the West End. She returned to Shropshire with her land surveyor husband to bring up their two children, and worked for Shropshire Libraries before training in garden design.

Her children's stories were broadcast on BBC TV's *Play School*, and her collection of Shropshire folk stories, *Witches & Warriors: Legends from the Shropshire Marches*, was published by Shropshire Books.

She published a series of crossword books on Shropshire, Gardening, and Literature under her imprint Beanpole Books and in 2005 published her first crime novel, *Death in the Physic Garden* introducing garden designer Fern Green. It had taken ten years to write. The sequel, *Death in the Winter Garden*, published in 2010, took a mere seven years to complete.

The Quilt Detective: a Patchwork of Poison was her first crafting murder mystery, inspired by her love of creative textiles. *Motif for Murder* is the second book in the series.

www.karenlowe.co.uk

1

ANGHARAD

Like black crows they stood there at the graveside, their shawls and coats flapping in that bitter wind. There was snow still lying, and the ground was hard. Hard digging to cut out a second grave, I thought. The minister's words swirled round us on the wind. I could not cry for the fear that gripped me. I glanced at Dafydd beside me. He stood head bowed, clasping his cap. All the while his gaze fixed with a stony fury on Father's open grave.

I slipped my hand through his arm. He shook free of me, would take no comfort. Without a backward glance he strode away down the path, heading for the horse and cart that had first carried our mother's coffin and now our father's. It was the last time he set foot in Bethesda Chapel.

I felt a light touch on my arm. I looked round into Sarah's sweet face.

'Come back with us to the farm. Mam's put on a spread.'

I shook my head. 'I'd better go with Dafydd,' I told her. 'He needs me now.'

'I'll see you at Chapel next Sunday then.' She made it sound like a question, as if none of us could be certain of anything any more.

How cold the stone farmhouse seemed now. Cold and silent. And there was nothing I could do to make it warm again. I was used to the work, to the harsh daily rhythm of the hill farm, but there had been comfort in it too. My mother made sure of that. I missed her smiles, and her singing. A fine voice for hymns she had. But the winter had done for them both. There were such snows, it was hard to get out to tend the stock. Father and Dafydd were away for hours, long after it was dark, checking on the animals, carrying fodder. After the last snowstorm, they'd had to search for the sheep, and dig them out of the drifts before they suffocated or starved. All the same, we lost six ewes. A bad winter. Then, at the end of January, Mam had taken to her bed with pneumonia and not all my care or prayers had been enough to save her. When she died, it broke Father's heart. Two weeks after, he fell ill himself, as if the fire had gone out in him. At nineteen, Dafydd was left to run the farm alone, with me, just sixteen, his only help.

I knew his anger had been brewing all week since the funeral. Knew it, but could do nothing about it. He watched me fasten on my Sunday bonnet and wrap Mam's thick shawl over my coat.

'Where do you think you're going?'

'To Chapel of course. Are you coming?' I knew the answer.

'I've work to do.'

'On a Sunday?' And I stared at him, frightened, knowing it was a sin to work on the Sabbath. But since our parents' death, he'd become bitter and angry. I heard it in the way he treated the poor beasts, and it made me sick to the heart for there was nothing I could do to soften him. I heard it in the way he slammed the door, saw him scowl at me whatever food I put in front of him. Nothing I did was ever right. Such dreadful things he said, about God punishing him unjustly. And as he raged, it seemed to me there was a light come into his eyes like the fires of Hell. Dafydd had always had his tempers, but nothing like these. It was as if he blamed God and me for what had happened.

'Who'll do the work if I don't?' he demanded. I shut my eyes, tried not to listen to his blasphemy. Now there was no Mam to sweeten him, or Da to scold him into line. For the first time I was afraid of him.

Every Sunday, waking in the cold dark bedroom, I'd have the same sick fear start inside me. It made me clumsy as I set the fire and made breakfast, trembling all the more as the time neared when I must put on my bonnet and shawl and walk down the valley to the Watkins' farm. I was always afraid he would fly into one of his rages, that he would stop me going. But when at last the beasts were fed and I could escape, I would almost run down the bank, along the path beside the river, to be blessed with Sarah's smile and walk beside her to Chapel, her brothers all dressed in their Sunday best following behind us. Such singing there was as we made our merry progress. They were good-hearted boys, and Mr and Mrs Watkins treated me like one of their own.

Sarah had always been my best friend. I loved nothing more than to be with her. There was little company for me at the farm with Dafydd and his rages. He'd always been a hard worker. Mucking out, carting fodder, ploughing, tilling: he'd done it all since he was a boy, and with Da gone he expected me to help him. Oh, I was strong, and used to hard work, but I couldn't keep up with him. I had the cows to milk, the pigs and hens to tend, and I'd to keep house and cook as well, and there was always such a tide of mud traipsed into the house. He didn't seem to understand.

Sarah's father must have seen how thin I'd grown, for he said I was welcome to come down to the farm on market day while Dafydd was away, and sit with Sarah and sew. We used to join them to sew when Mam was alive. Only now, with our parents gone, there always so much work. But I told Dafydd I could get more money by selling the quilts I made and so he was content for me to go.

Oh, they were lovely days. For a while even Dafydd seemed happy. He said that Sarah was a fine companion for me A pretty thing, she was, very demure. At first he'd call for me in the cart on his way home from market, and it seemed as if something about the life and the people at market had eased his troubles. But soon it came that he was staying longer and later at market, and when he stopped by, I could smell the drink on his breath. I didn't want him to come in and speak to the Watkins then. I was ashamed of him, and I felt guilty for that, for his life was hard now and he had no comfort else. I took to leaving early, before Dafydd came home, and Sarah's youngest brother would walk with me back along the valley and up the hill to the farm. It was a pretty enough walk in fair weather, for the path followed alongside the river, and we'd see kingfishers sometimes, and black-and-white dipping birds on the stones. It wasn't far, a shorter walk than going round by the road, but it was lonely when the days were short, and I was glad of his company. I was fond of him. Dafydd said he was soft in the head; *twp*, he called him. He was nineteen, and his mother's favourite. Of all Sarah's brothers, he was the kindest and gentlest. And he was fond of me. He was always smiling and his eyes shone with a merry light. It was as if he was all sunshine while Dafydd was all darkness. How could the two ever have been friends?

That Easter, he turned twenty. He took to coming in early from the fields when I was there sewing with Sarah. When his brothers came in, there'd be laughing and shouting, and they'd look in at us as we sat together in the front parlour, and tease us, and hide our thimbles. But he was content to sit quietly beside us and watch us sewing. We made some fine quilts, sold some of them too. The quilt patterns were just as our mothers and grandmothers had taught us: scrolls and scissors and twisted cables. One day he watched us chalk out a pattern on a quilt top, ready to stitch. He said he could make a better one for us. We just laughed; we didn't believe him. What did he know about drawing? But the next week when I went to the farm, he brought me a sketch he'd made. It was two rose stems and leaves, curved round to make a heart. And in the centre of the heart were our initials, A and E. From the way he looked at me, I knew he wanted me for his sweetheart. But how was I going to tell Dafydd?

I wouldn't let him walk me home that day, but I hid the drawing inside my prayer book. I knew Dafydd would not find it there. It was as if all the hardships since our parents died had been a trial, and now I was to be rewarded, for that was how it felt when I thought of Elis. I would go to live with him on the farm, and have Sarah always as my sister. I'd never felt so happy. Yet I said nothing to Dafydd. I don't know if he suspected anything. I was so happy then, that even when he railed at me, I didn't mind. But when I went to Chapel that Sunday, I saw my brother up on the hill, watching like a wolf as I walked with Sarah, and Elis close by.

The next market day, when I went to Watkins' farm, Elis was waiting for me. He asked me what I thought of the design, if it suited me, and so I told him plainly, it suited me very well. And I knew then that he meant to marry me.

Sarah knew what Elis was thinking, even without his saying, and she said we must make a new quilt, one for our marriage bed, even if it wouldn't be needed for a while yet. We collected all the prettiest scraps we could find. There was a handsome print of roses in a vase that

9

2

BRONWEN

MONDAY

February Fill-dyke was living up to its name. The rain had not relented in days. Through the torrent, the Land Rover's windscreen wipers barely cleared a view of a landscape dissolving into liquid grey. By four, the daylight was all but snuffed out like a damp firework. The gloom deepened as I drove along the narrow lane, its high banks rising towards dark woodland. As I rounded the bend, I saw red lights glimmer wetly. There was a car stopped in the middle of the lane. I braked, slithering to a halt in the mud. Peering through the rivulets of water I could see in the headlights' beam a hump of black land and the reaching silhouette of branches. The road, it seemed, had vanished. There'd been a landslip, I realised; it had brought down one of the trees from the woods. And the car in front of me had just run into it.

Hunched in my jacket, I ran over to the car. The VW Beetle's engine was still running, but the bonnet was wedged beneath the overhanging branches. The huge tree was tilted head first down the bank of mud that had engulfed the road.

'Are you OK?'

A small white face stared up at me from the driver's seat, her breath misting the pane. Her hands still gripped the steering wheel. She gave a stiff uncertain nod.

'Are you hurt?' I asked her.

'I… I don't think so,' she said, shivering. She looked about twenty. Cropped dark hair above an elfin face, and dark eyes wide with shock.

I heard the loud crack of wood. The tree groaned, shuddered a little. Heart racing, I glanced back at its great dark bulk.

'It's not safe here. Come and sit in my car. I'll ring for help.'

She didn't move. 'Bryn will bloody kill me,' she said.

'Not if the tree gets you first,' I said. 'Come on.'

With the girl safe beside me in the Land Rover, I cautiously reversed back around the bend and switched on the hazard lights. As I reached for my phone to call the police, I shuddered. Not shock, exactly. It was just that, as I'd backed away from the landslip, the headlights had swung across the bank of earth. And in their slow trajectory, over the tumble of rocks, mud and tree roots, I had seen a rounded stone that gleamed paler than the rest. With two dark indents like eye sockets, it had looked exactly like a skull.

'My name's Bron,' I said as we waited for the police to arrive. 'Bronwen Jones.'

'Rachel,' she said in a thin small voice.

'So who's Bryn then?' I asked. 'Boyfriend?'

She nodded.

'He'll be glad you're not hurt,' I said. She gave me a disparaging glance.

'The Beetle's his baby,' she said. 'I didn't ask if I could borrow it. Spends days doing it up, he does. The chrome and paintwork's immaculate. Was,' she corrected, tearfully. 'I had to go and see my friend, Magda, but my Mini's got a flat battery. So I took the Beetle. Bryn doesn't know yet.'

'You'd better ring and tell him what's happened,' I said. 'Tell him you're OK. He'll need to get the car picked up, and get you home. Where do you live?'

'Nantmawr. It's only a few miles from here.'

'I'm on my way back to Bishop's Castle. This was supposed to be a shortcut from Llannon, across country,' I said with a sigh. A journey that should have taken three quarters of an hour at most. Didn't look now as if I'd be home for hours. I was starting to feel hungry. Must be the effect of shock, I thought. Mind, it didn't take much to make me feel hungry; just breathing seemed to do it. Which was why I'd never be a slight elfin creature like Rachel.

'Sorry,' she said miserably.

'Not your fault,' I said. 'It's all the rain we've had.'

'Bloody hell!' she said, opening the door. 'I've got to go back. Magda's stuff – it's still in the car.' She was out of the Land Rover before I could stop her.

'Rachel, wait! Be careful!' Poor kid. She looked more scared of what the boyfriend would say than shocked by the accident. I decided I'd drop her home and maybe stick around till Bryn showed up, just to make sure she was all right. I risked a glance at the mud slide again. No sign of the skull now. Perhaps I'd imagined it.

'She'd have killed me if anything had happened to this lot,' Rachel said, out of breath as she lugged the box back to the car.

'She'd have to join the queue then, wouldn't she?' I said.

She gave a hesitant smile.

'Can't blame her. You should see the jewellery she makes,' she said as she stowed the box on the back seat. 'Bracelets, glass beads, and the most gorgeous buttons, like little sweeties.'

'Buttons?' I turned towards the box like a hound catching a scent.

'Yes. I sell them for her. I've got a stall at Llannon market, three days a week. The Button Box.'

'I'm always on the look-out for something new,' I said. 'I'm a textile artist. And as of today, officially Quilter in Residence with Llannon library service. Not the most auspicious start, is it?' I said ruefully. 'I'd love to come and see your stall next time I'm in town.'

'Wednesday, Friday, Saturday,' she said. She rummaged in her bag and gave me a card. 'It's got my email address on it. Magda really needs the money. She's got a kiddie. Only ten months he is, but you know how things are,' she said with a shrug. I nodded. I didn't, of course, not having had children. Nor ever would. 'So what do you do then, as Quilter in Residence?'

'Talks, workshops and research,' I said. 'Just for six months.' I would put my own life and career as a textile artist on hold till then. Not that it would be difficult. There was precious little to give up. I was over forty, overweight, and there hadn't been a man in my life since my divorce four years ago. Not counting Gabriel, of course. But could I even count him? Where was he now? I hadn't heard from him since Christmas. 'The project's called "Every quilt tells a story".'

It was Llannon's heritage in the wool industry that was the start of the story. There'd been dozens of flannel and tweed mills there in its heyday. The flannel they produced was much in demand for its softness next to the skin. Almost every farm and cottage around had been involved in the process: carding, weaving, spinning.

'I'm hoping to unearth some antique quilts from the area for the exhibition we're holding in the museum in

14

July,' I told her. 'I'd like to display the heirloom quilts alongside the ones we produce in the workshops. Past and present together.'

'Sounds a great idea,' she said. 'About time something happened in Llannon.'

In the mirror I saw blue flashing lights approaching. A police car drew up behind us. I wound down the window just enough to avoid the worst of the rain.

'The bank's given way and there's a tree down, blocking the road,' I said. 'Rachel drove into it. Her car's there under the branches.'

The young policeman nodded, flinching under the battering of rain and wind.

'Anyone hurt?'

'No, thankfully. But I need to get her home. She's cold and wet through.'

'If I could just take a few details first, Miss,' he said.

While I answered his questions, Rachel took out her mobile to try and get through to Bryn again. I could hear her explaining, pleading, as she told him he'd have to get someone to pick up the damaged car. At least with an engine at the rear of the car, it might still be driveable.

'There's something else,' I told the policeman. 'Up on the bank where the tree's come down, I thought I saw a skull.'

He gave a tired smile.

'A sheep, I expect,' he said in his soothing Welsh lilt. 'Get used to that round here. Always escaping, getting stuck, sheep. Got a death wish, my old man reckons.'

'Yes. Of course.' I looked into his smiling face and persuaded myself he was right. Nothing to worry about.

'You go. I'll be OK,' Rachel said as she finished her call. 'Bryn's on his way. He's getting a lift from the pub.'

'If you're sure? I can wait if you want me to.'

She nodded, looking as small and scared as ever.

'I'm sure.'

I watched her make her way towards the police car carrying her box of beads. Cautiously I turned the Land Rover in the narrow lane and edged past the police car. I pulled up, lowering my window.

'I'll be in Llannon Wednesday. I'll come and see you in the market,' I said.

'Yes. Do come. See you then,' she said brightly.

I retreated towards the main road but did not look back. It wasn't just Rachel I was worried about. I pictured the landslip and that distinctive domed shape with its dark eye sockets. Much as I wanted to believe PC Roberts, to feel relief and reassurance, I very much doubted it had been a sheep at all.

3

TUESDAY

It had been Vi, my near neighbour down the lane at Apple Tree Cottage, who had seen the advert. Quilters and crafters were invited to apply for the post of Quilter in Residence based in Llannon library, over the Welsh border. I knew it would leave me little time for my own work, but February and March were always lean months for sales, and Clive Rednal, the gallery owner in Ludlow who showcased my art quilts, was away in Barbados. I still had one quilt to complete, though, and the deadline for that was fast approaching: a wall hanging for the new visitor centre in the Clun Forest. The launch was barely two weeks away.

I studied the large pinboard on the studio wall. It was covered with swatches of fabric and scraps of ribbon, as well as sketches and photographs, most of them prompting ideas for the quilt. The quilt was close to being finished, but there was a great deal of surface detail still to add, and most of that work had to be done by hand: sewing buttons and sequins, adding decorative stitching, building up layers of texture and light. On that bleak grey morning it was hard to summon any enthusiasm for my work. From the wide bay window of the studio, I looked out at the alluring view of the hills and valleys of the Welsh marches. I dropped my coffee mug into the sink and reached for my car keys.

I climbed into the Land Rover and set off down the lane. Turning onto the main road, I headed south, splashing through the mud and standing water, towards Clun Forest, just six miles away from my cottage on the hillside above Bishop's Castle.

It was four years since my divorce. After Ed and I had sold the house and he'd bought my share of the landscape gardening business we'd built up together, I had moved into Ceri Cottage with enough money to renovate it to provide the studio space I needed, and, with care, enough to live on until I had established a career in textile art. Along the crest of the hill behind the cottage ran an ancient track, the Kerry Ridgeway, which led for fifteen miles from South Shropshire into Wales. It had been a trade route for centuries. The hills around were littered with Iron Age tumuli, standing stones, ditches and castle mounds, so many traces of previous inhabitants, long-vanished ways of life. Yet for all its solitude, I had never felt alone in the cottage. I had worked to build up Ed's business and now for the first time I had the chance to develop my own creativity, and I loved every minute of it.

As I pulled up in the mire that passed for a car park, I could see two stocky men in high-visibility jackets and hardhats standing before the green oak frame that would shortly be transformed into the Clun Forest Visitor Centre. Inside, my quilt would be hung on display to welcome the Centre's visitors. If all went to plan. I sighed, briefly submerging beneath the weight of dread, expectation and self-doubt.

'Bron, come to check up on us?' Elwyn called as he caught sight of me at the safety barriers.

'It's looking great,' I lied. If I'd been daunted at the thought of all I still had to do, how must he feel, as site manager, knowing the windows weren't yet glazed, and, judging by the quantity of white spaghetti-like wires sprouting from the walls, the electrics weren't finished either? At least the roof was on, though not yet planted with the proposed grasses and sedums. The opening was barely two weeks away. It would be a race to see which of us would be ready first. It was one race I almost didn't want to win.

'Think you'll be ready in time?' I said, trying not to wince.

'No choice really,' he said.

I squinted up at him under the steady pattering of raindrops. 'This rain can't help.'

'Welsh builders,' he said mildly, unflappable as ever. 'Wouldn't have it any other way. Wouldn't know what to do in blazing sunshine, would we Dai?'

Dai muttered something inaudible and clumped off into the building, thick brown mud plastering his boots.

I gave Elwyn as cheery a smile as I could muster.

'Think I'll stick to quilting,' I said. 'Thought I'd just come for a walk. Get a bit of enthusiasm sparked before I start on the last leg of the wall hanging.'

'See you at the launch then,' he called after me as I trudged down the path into the forest.

The Forest Trust, custodians of the new Visitor Centre, had chosen my design for the wall hanging because they had already seen my quilt series inspired by the ancient chestnut trees at Croft Castle. But the design for Clun Forest had to weave in something of the forest's folklore. According to legend, in these ancient woodlands lived the beautiful elf-maidens, the Lady Godda and her sisters. One day, when the nobleman Wild Edric was out hunting in the forest, he lost his way. After wandering for some time, he saw the lights of a great house in the distance, and drawing near, saw the tall and graceful Godda dancing in a ring with her sisters, and fell instantly in love with her. For three days he tried to persuade her to come away with him as his bride, but without success. Then, on the fourth day, she relented, but on one condition. He would have happiness and wealth as long as he never said an ill word against her sisters or the place she had come from. And so they rode away and lived happily ever after. Until, that is, the day he came home late from hunting and couldn't find Godda anywhere. When she finally appeared, he told her angrily, 'I suppose you've been away with your sisters.' At which point, she disappeared, his fortune dwindled, and he pined away broken-hearted.

I wondered what Ed, my ex-husband, would make of the legend. A promise betrayed. Although in his case it was rather more calculating. Another woman. The baby they had produced, while he and I had made a bargain not to have children until his business was established. Oh, not that I thought men had sole rights to deceit and duplicity. Last summer's tragedy, set in train by Gabriel Haywood's beautiful self-centred daughter Lydia, had been a bitter lesson in the power of beauty to destroy as well as inspire. But the legend had so many echoes, about power and trust, and love and forgiveness or the want of it. It was hard to sustain that light, airy, magical quality to the quilt, knowing what was to happen. Perhaps that sense of foreboding was sewn into most of folklore: the darkness of the forests, losing one's way. I glanced nervously back over my shoulder, noting the waymarkers, making sure I was keeping to the right path. At least there were no wolves lurking in the undergrowth. As far as I knew.

It was difficult, in the rain-sodden gloom of the forest, to remember how I had felt when I had first visited the forest to gain inspiration for my design. There was no birdsong now, just the steady drip and patter of rain through bare branches. And the dank earthy scent of fungi hung in the air, redolent of death and decay. A leaning trunk gave a roof-like outline for an elvish house. All it wanted was a slender shaft of sunlight to mimic the light from its windows. Fat chance. The rain fell more steadily, cold on my face. It was going to need an effort of imagination to give the woodland quilt that illusion of light and magic.

It was late lunchtime by the time I returned to Bishop's Castle. I'd taken the slow route home, driving through Horderley just for old times' sake, passing right by the gates of Cropstone Hall, Gabriel's country retreat from his hectic life as an investment banker in the City. It was over a month since I'd heard from him, and then it had been just a Christmas card, signed with his beautifully abandoned scrawl, 'Fond memories, with love, Gabriel'. Valentine's Day had come and gone without a repeat. Now I knew why.

I drove up the steep lane towards my cottage at the end of the track, and stopped outside Vi's to drop off the sack of dog food I'd picked up for her in town. I hoped she'd been baking; I was in urgent need of something gooey and chocolatey. As I opened the door into the kitchen, I was overwhelmed with a rich sweet scent. There it was, cooling on the rack, one of Vi's deep dark concoctions: a chocolate fudge cake.

'Vi, you're a mind reader,' I told her, dumping the sack of dog food. Her little Jack Russell, William, skittered across the kitchen and danced round me with an enthusiasm of barking and stumpy tail-wagging I only wished I could imitate. That was just how the cake made me feel.

'Tough morning?' she asked, her head cocked bird-like to one side. She was wearing a long purple cardigan over a vivid floral blouse, and cream flares. Vi had abandoned her sober grey suits the day she retired from accountancy, and reverted with gusto to the

21

kaftans, paisleys and pop-art she'd adored in her younger days.

'Mm,' I said, my glance returning longingly to the cake.

I heard her fill the kettle at the sink and then the clink of two mugs. I peeled off my anorak and sat down at the table.

'You going to tell me about it?'

I took a sip of coffee. The heat and steam filled my face, smarted in my eyes. I blinked hard.

'It's Gabriel,' I said. 'Cropstone Hall is up for sale. That means he's not coming back.'

'Getting on with his life. You said you understood that.'

'I know what I said,' I responded. 'Only now that I know he's made up his mind to live somewhere else…' I faltered, afraid that any minute I'd start crying. Which was stupid. Vi was right, of course. I'd accepted that a man like Gabriel Haywood, good-looking, wealthy, with a beautiful ex-wife in the States, and used to a high-flying lifestyle as an investment banker, was never going to settle for a sleepy Shropshire hamlet and an overweight forty-something divorcee like me. All the same, I realised now only too keenly, I had not given up hoping. Stupidly. Look where it had got me. Struggling not to dissolve into tears like a love-struck teenager. It wasn't as if I'd been looking for another man in my life. I wasn't entirely out of love with Ed, truth to tell, no matter that I felt betrayed and embittered. You don't stop loving someone overnight. Until I met Gabriel, that is. Strange how quickly he'd become an antidote to my yearning for Ed.

'Oh, Bron,' Vi sighed. 'You poor thing. I never guessed you were so smitten.'

'I'm not,' I insisted. 'It was just, you know, that glimmer of hope. That there could be someone in my life again. I mean, he never gave me any reason to think… He's never even kissed me!' I said with a bitter laugh. I wished it wasn't true. Hadn't I fantasised about it far too often? Melting into his strong arms, gazing up into his dark eyes. I sighed.

Vi looked sternly at me.

'I should have guessed something like this would happen. You've spent far too long on your own in the cottage, drooling over Gabriel while you're sewing. It's a jolly good thing you've got the library job. It'll get you out and about. And high time too.'

'Now you're making me sound pathetic. Desperate for a man.'

'I know that's not true,' she said with a little more sympathy. 'But sometimes things can get out of proportion. You said yourself, Gabriel gave you no indication that he felt anything other than friendship. You have to face up to that, and get on with your life.'

'I know,' I sighed. I pushed my plate away. 'Thanks for the chocolate cake. And the telling-off. I needed both.'

Back home in Ceri Cottage, I busied myself in the kitchen, cutting two thick slices of wholemeal bread and grilling bacon for a sandwich. A very late lunch, but I was starving, despite the cake. Vi was right of course. I knew it myself. One Christmas card since Gabriel had gone back to London in the autumn did not indicate a nascent passion of any kind. I sat at the table in my kitchen living room, and glared up at the chirpy robin on the card I had left in place on the shelf.

'Fondest love, indeed,' I snorted. Wasn't that something you wrote to maiden aunts? I got up and retrieved Gabriel's Christmas card, and determinedly tore it into confetti, and scattered it into the bin. I can't say it made me feel any better, though.

I had just poured a second mug of tea when there came a sharp rap at the door. Too late for the postman. A courier, perhaps, with the fabrics I'd ordered? I marched barefoot down the hall.

'Oh,' I said. And despite my forty-odd years of linguistic competence, could not think of another word to say. I stared up at Gabriel, conscious only that there was a smear of bacon grease on my chin, and probably a hint of tomato ketchup.

Gabriel frowned slightly. Perhaps he could see the bacon grease too.

'Hi Bron. Sorry, I should have phoned first but I don't have much time,' he said gruffly.

'Oh?'

He shuffled awkwardly, glanced back at the sleek Jaguar XKR parked at my gate.

'Mind if I come in?'

'No. Of course not. I've just made a pot of tea,' I burbled, backing away from him. 'I'll get you a mug. Sorry there's no cake.'

By the time I reached the kitchen, my cheeks were glowing. I gave my chin a surreptitious wipe on my sleeve. Mug in hand, I drew a deep steadying breath, and turned to face him with a forced smile.

'So you're leaving us, I see,' I said.

'Ah, you saw the 'For Sale' board. I meant to tell you.' His frown deepened. 'I didn't want you to think I was running away,' he said with a vain effort at a laugh.

'There's nothing to explain. I mean, it's your life,' I said airily.

Carefully he took the mug from me as if it were something precious, fragile. I found my gaze lingering on the curl of his strong tanned fingers, his broad hands.

'It's not the way I wanted it to end,' he said.

'Oh.' So it was the end. I hadn't really thought it had ever started. I looked round for my mug. Anything rather than meet his eyes. I could not let him see the misery I felt. The collapse of all my hopes.

'Lydia's given up her place at Cambridge. It's got to her: guilt at what happened. She's gone to stay with her mother in the States for a while. Annabel and I, well, we're hoping we can work this through together, for Lydia's sake.'

'Of course.' I refused to say anything judgemental about his daughter or the way he had handled her behaviour. He looked like that was the last thing he needed.

'You asked me before if she was contrite,' he said, his expression tense, almost mask-like. 'Fact is, she's taken it rather hard.'

Not before time, I thought.

'I'm sorry,' I said, and it was true. I could see now the strain in his face, the shadows beneath his eyes. I realised he hadn't really smiled once since he'd turned up on my doorstep. Where was the old Gabriel, with that beguiling charm? Was he to be another of Lydia's victims, abandoning himself, his life, for her sake?

'There seems little point keeping the house on here. Understandably she never wants to go back there again. I've no idea how long we'll be away. I have to be there for Lydia, however long that takes.'

'Of course.'

'I need to decide what furniture to keep. There'll be quite a lot going to auction. My agent will see to all that. I have to be back in London tonight. A lot of loose ends to tie up. All business, I'm afraid. I'm not going out to the States for a couple of weeks. Didn't want to miss the Clun launch. The new Visitor Centre. You are coming, aren't you?' he asked earnestly.

'Yes, of course. I'd hardly miss that. They're unveiling my wall hanging,' I said, wondering why the Forest Centre was so important to him.

'Yes, so they are. How could I forget,' he muttered. He set down his mug next to mine. I saw he'd hardly drunk any of his tea. It was as if he wished he were somewhere else. With Lydia, no doubt. 'That's good. I'll see you then. It'll be good... No, no,' he said crossly. 'It won't be good at all. Bron, it'll be my last chance to say goodbye.'

When he looked at me, I saw only anguish in his eyes. A raw pain, which I had no idea how to help or heal.

'You can always come and visit,' I said evenly, although my heart was pounding, my stomach knotting itself into a tangle.

He dismissed my words with a shake of his head. He drew closer, his eyes fixed on mine as if hypnotised.

'I wanted to belong here. To be part of your life,' he said with an effort.

'My life?' I faltered.

'Is that such a surprise?' he said.

'Well, yes. It is rather.'

'Then I expect this will be too,' he said as his arms encircled me and pulled me closer against him. His head dipped to mine, as with a shuddering sigh, he kissed me.

Somehow I didn't faint, though I didn't breathe for quite some time. And when he did draw away, it was only to look anxiously into my face, unsure of my reaction. It was far better than anything I had imagined.

'Are you always this good at goodbyes?' I said, breathless.

He did not answer. His body seemed to surround me, his hands gently gliding over the contours of my body. Light-headed, I clung to him. How had I managed to fool myself for so long? Of course I was in love with him. A fierce desire fizzed through me, reckless, unafraid. I wanted him to hold me tightly against him, to feel his skin naked against mine. And he wanted me.

'Bron,' he groaned. 'This isn't what I wanted. I just have no choice.'

'I know, I know,' I whispered. 'I understand.'

As his lips found mine again, with that eager hunger of desire, I heard his phone ring.

Gabriel hesitated. Would he ignore it?

'Sorry,' he said. 'I really should take this.'

He retreated towards the French doors, straightening his shirt as he pulled the phone from his pocket.

'Hi sweetheart. How's it going?'

I drank my tea and waited impatiently. I heard him call her 'Liddy'. So it was his daughter. Perfect timing, I thought cynically.

'I should be going anyway,' he said, returning to me as he ended the call.

He glanced away, unfocused. Lydia's call had evidently brought back too many memories. He felt uncomfortable now.

'Liddy needs me,' he said, his voice hoarse. 'I can't let her down again.'

Again? So was he blaming himself for his daughter's selfishness? For the contempt with which she had treated the gifted young man who had idolised her? I felt a sudden flare of anger. Didn't he see? She had no right to go on messing up other people's lives. She had to learn.

He turned back to me then, anguish in his face.

'After Christmas, Liddy was due to fly back to Milan. I found her,' he said. 'She'd tried to kill herself. An overdose. The guilt, you see. She just couldn't deal with it. I have to be there for her.'

I nodded dumbly. Of course he had to be with his daughter. I was the one being selfish, wanting to keep him here, wanting him for myself. And, oh, how I wanted him. I sighed and reached out my hand, and touched his cheek.

'I can wait,' I said.

4

WEDNESDAY

Exactly what Gabriel had meant by 'we're hoping we can work this through together' continued to torment me through the night and into the following morning. It was like a nagging toothache. He was divorced, wasn't he? Surely Lydia's problems weren't going to be the catalyst to bring Gabriel and his ex-wife back together? All the same, it had me worried. Waiting for him to come back, however long that might take, was one thing, but I knew exactly what Vi would say about me moping over a lost cause. He was selling the house. How much stronger a message did I need that he had no intention of coming back here to me?

I accelerated, as if trying to outrun the crowding doubts. I had my work, which I loved, my freedom, and, until yesterday, some kind of peace of mind. That had been hard won. It was stupid to throw it all away so lightly. Though love, I'd found, had a horrible habit of complicating everything.

I reached Llannon at nine-thirty, just as the library was opening. The little town had once been at the heart of the Montgomeryshire wool trade. The handsome half-timbered building in the centre had for centuries been a bustling market for fleece and flannel, but now served as a museum, closed half the week. Beside the town ran the fast flowing river that had once been used to wash fleeces and power its mills and machinery, but the last of the flannel mills stood derelict. Industry had moved on, and left Llannon behind.

'*Every quilt tells a story*'. The poster greeted me as I pushed open the library door. My first workshop was due to start at ten. I set up a table with a basket of ready-cut patchwork scraps, and a selection of coloured thread. Kate, the librarian, brought me coffee. She was near my own age, with curly brown hair tinged with grey, and dark-framed spectacles. Her long grey knitted cardigan clung to her comfortably rounded hips.

'Not many booked for this morning,' she said with an apologetic smile. 'Early days though. They'll soon get to know you're here.'

'This weather doesn't help,' I said. 'I saw the Penwern road was still closed after the landslip.'

I tipped out the patchwork pieces I planned to make up into a quilt of geometric blocks: a bow-tie design in traditional colours of red, grey, and black, just as the Welsh quilters had once pieced flannel from scarlet petticoats and worn-out woollens. Stuffed with sheep's wool, the quilts would have been heavy and thick, and made for warm bedding. Too thick for anything but the simplest of quilting patterns.

A pink-faced woman with a short bob of grey hair approached. She was clutching a bulging carrier bag, her black patent-leather handbag slung on a gold chain over her shoulder.

'Have you come for the workshop?' I asked, with what I hoped was an inviting smile.

'I'm not sure,' she began. 'Could you do something with these?'

I peered into the bag she held out. Inside was a jumble of colours and patterns. Silks, by the look of them.

'My husband's ties,' she said. 'I saw your poster. About the stories.'

'You've got plenty of fabric,' I said, encouraging. 'Why don't you sit down? We'll see what we can come up with.'

She sat down, the bag on her lap.

'Hugh always took such pride in his appearance,' she said. He wasn't the only one, I thought. She was smartly dressed in a black belted raincoat over a white cowl-necked jumper. 'It's been six months now since… since he passed away. I thought, it's time.'

Gently I took the bag from her and lifted out a handful of the ties. The slips of gold, navy, pink, rustled between my fingers. Stripes, spots, paisleys: it would need care to make the vibrant colours and patterns harmonise.

'A keepsake quilt, is that what you were thinking?'

Her eyes widened in alarm.

'It doesn't have to be a big piece,' I added hastily. 'Cushions. How about making a cushion?' There was probably enough fabric for a dozen cushions, but I didn't dare suggest it. I selected one or two of the ties in complementary colours: a navy stripe, a lemon paisley, a rich gold. 'Look how good these are together. They'll look stunning.'

'I can't do anything complicated,' she said doubtfully. 'I was going to take them to the charity shop, then I saw the poster. Well, they do tell a story, don't they? I mean, I can remember where I bought most of them. And remember him wearing them. Be a shame just to let it all go.'

'Just pick out a few of your favourites. His favourites,' I said. 'We can team them up with some plainer pieces. If we press the fabric open we can cut out a few rectangles and join them up in a log-cabin pattern. Look.' I showed her one of the samples I'd pinned on the board behind the table. 'Doesn't even have to be a cushion. Nine blocks, say, and you could frame it as a picture.'

For the first time her anxious expression eased a little.

31

'Yes,' she said. 'A cushion would be nice. I think maybe I could manage that.'

'We're going to have an exhibition in the museum in July. It would be great to have something like this on display. A story to tell.'

'I could tell you a few stories about Hugh,' she said, smiling. 'Right then.' She tipped up the bag and poured the rest of the ties out onto the table. 'Where do we start?'

Ann Cadwallader, as she introduced herself, took up a pair of scissors and began unpicking the ties and flattening them out. 'I think I'm going to enjoy this,' she said.

It was almost twelve by the time Ann left and I began to pack away the scrap pieces. The library was busier now: women with shopping bags, trailing toddlers, a couple of schoolchildren giggling at one of the computer screens. A young woman came to study the display board where I'd pinned up my patchwork patterns.

'I'm doing another workshop on Friday if you want to come along,' I said.

She gave a shrug of her narrow shoulders. She was small and slim, late teens, early twenties. Her long hair was dyed a dark red that made her face look all the paler.

'I'll be gone by then,' she said.

'Well, another time maybe. I'm here for six months.'

'She looked keen,' she said, nodding in the direction Ann had gone.

'She lost her husband. She kept all his ties, so she's going to make a keepsake cushion with them.'

'She should chuck it all out. Make a fresh start,' she said. 'Move on. That's my motto.'

Her eyes as they fixed on me were an icy blue. I had the feeling she would not be easy to get close to. Moving on, putting distance between her and whatever had gone wrong, was her way of dealing with life. I suppose I could understand that. After all, I'd done much the same thing after I'd found out about my ex and his new girlfriend, the duplicitous Miranda. Taken my share of the money and headed for the hills. Well, the Welsh marches, at least. Nothing to remind me of the life in Surrey we'd once had. And the child he had had with Miranda. The Tulip, I called her, remembering the excruciating moment I had seen the baby in the pushchair at the shopping mall, its face goblet-shaped, its cheeks red and shiny. I'd been glad it wasn't a pretty child. Ed didn't deserve it. I had wanted so badly to punish him.

It wasn't easy though. Some part of me did still love him and want to forgive him. I wanted to hear him say he'd been a fool, made a mistake he bitterly regretted. Only now there was the child. She must be four years old. That was something I couldn't give him. And couldn't forgive him for.

'Some people do find them a comfort: keepsakes, memory quilts,' I said. Hadn't I hung on to some of Ed's gardening books? Reaching them down from the shelf, I had often held them, pictured him poring over them with his long strong fingers.

'You do a lot of memory quilts then?'

She wasn't pretty exactly, there was too much sharpness in her features for that, but still, her wide-eyed gaze and high cheekbones compelled attention.

'Not very often. But I'm here to teach others how to make them. They can use what they've got at home. Favourite clothes the children have outgrown. Scraps of old fabric. All the things you can never quite throw away.'

'Can't abide a lot of clutter,' she said. 'Baggage, mental or physical, just slows you down. Gets in your way.'

'As they say, the best things in life aren't things,' I said.

She gave a fleeting wintery smile.

'If you want more fabric for your workshops, I've got a bag of stuff out on my bike. I was going to drop them off at the recycling.'

'Thanks,' I said. 'It'll come in useful. The local primary school are going to make something for the exhibition so we'll need plenty of material.'

'I'll fetch them for you.'

'You sure you don't want to join the workshop and make something yourself?'

'I don't want more stuff,' she said with disdain. 'Besides, I'll be long gone by then.'

By the time I had finished clearing my sewing away and sorting out with Kate the times for the next workshops, the red-haired girl had come back, this time carrying a black plastic bin bag. Her small strong fingers untied the bag. I peered in and saw printed cottons in bold blues and pinks, tie-dyed swirls, lace trims, beaded strips.

'Must be fun, cutting it all up to make something new,' she said. 'Like a jigsaw. I used to like jigsaws,' she said, almost wistful. So she hadn't quite moved on from everything, I thought.

'Are all these yours then?' I asked her.

She gave a shake of her head. 'Like I said, some people just hang on to stuff. Move on. Set yourself free.'

'Well, if you're sure you don't want them.'

She gave a brief smile showing small, even teeth.

'Time they were put to good use.'

I took the bag out to my car and stowed it in the boot. I just had time to get a sandwich and then see Rachel at The Button Box in the market. I was due at the primary school at two, to set up a simple patchwork project for the children. I needed sustenance. Children were not my speciality; I was dreading it. But it was part of my brief and too late to get out of now.

I found a café in the main street, The Daisy Chain, which was both vegetarian and organic. I felt healthier just walking in the door. I ordered a brie, pear and honey wholegrain roll, and a square of gooey chocolate brownie to follow, and sat at a table in the window. Across the street I could see the newsagent's board with the bold headline, '*Landslip closes road.*' Nothing about skeletons being unearthed though. I wondered if the police had found any more bones in the mud. Had I imagined seeing that skull? It had been dark, after all. Even if there had been bones, it was probably just a dead sheep, as PC Roberts had suggested. They must come across them all the time.

Llannon's Victorian market was a handsome building with a colonnaded entrance and a fine wrought iron balcony above. I could just imagine some Victorian bigwig in top hat and frock coat standing up there to spout worthy speeches to the gathered crowd. I made my way through the lunchtime shoppers, past stalls of piled *bara brith* and Welsh cakes, neat pyramids of fruit, arrays of leeks and carrots, and saw the painted board on the back wall: 'The Button Box'. The stall, however, was empty, just a bare table. On the adjoining stall were piles of small T-shirts, baskets of knitted toys and babies' booties in sugared almond colours. Beside them I saw a pair of tiny lace-up boots in pink suede. I felt my throat tighten, my cheeks flame. All I could think of was Ed's new baby, the Tulip. And that agonising mindless moment four Christmases ago when I had followed his beloved Miranda round the shopping mall. I had stood in the heat and bustle and the jangling carols, and had almost, almost, stolen his child.

'Cute, aren't they?'

I heard the woman's voice as if from a distance. I blinked, and looked round at her. The stall holder was watching me intently, with a bright hopeful smile. I backed away a step.

'I was looking for someone,' I said, knowing my cheeks were still scarlet. Did I look guilty? Did she think I was a shoplifter? 'The bead stall,' I said, with a nod at the empty table. 'The girl who runs it. Rachel. I thought she'd be here today.'

'Funny you should ask,' the woman said. 'She's always here. Never misses usually.'

'I was worried, that was all,' I said. 'There was an accident. The landslip up on the Penwern road, you know? She ran into it in her car, just before I came along. She was OK,' I added quickly, 'but she did look shaken up. I said I'd look in today and see how she was.'

'Well,' said the woman, studying the empty table-top. 'There's your answer. Poor Rachel. Doesn't have much luck, does she?'

'I was after some beads for my quilting,' I said. 'I'm working up at the library a few days a week. Quilter in Residence.' I smiled more confidently. The woman nodded.

'I heard. There's a few of my customers into patchwork and quilting. They make little cot quilts. So cute. Maybe I should get a few in to sell.'

'You don't happen to know Rachel's phone number, do you? She gave me her card with her email address, but there's no number on it.'

'I don't, sorry. I know where she lives, though. Gave her a lift home once when her car wouldn't start.'

The children at Llannon primary school behaved beautifully, give or take the occasional groan by some of the bigger boys who thought sewing was definitely girls' work, and would doubtlessly have preferred kicking a football to death. That said, they were keen to go out and forage for sheep's wool from the hedgerows, though it was likely that most of the children either lived on or near a sheep farm, given how many there were scattered over the hills and valleys around the little town. As well as the history project on Llannon's old flannel mills, which their teachers were arranging, I asked them to design their own patchwork block that we would piece together to make a big quilt, and showed them some of the traditional patterns, with central diamonds and triangles, and wide borders.

I left the little school and found my way through the lanes back towards the main Newtown road. I stopped at the crossroads and studied the signpost. Nantmawr. Rachel's home. If I turned left instead of right, I could maybe see her, and make sure she was OK.

Nantmawr wasn't so much a village as a row of terraced cottages and a farm. There was little in the way of amenities apart from a postbox. It wasn't hard to work out which house Rachel lived in. Only one had a muddy VW Beetle in the drive, under a shroud of plastic.

There was a light on in the front room. I wondered if Bryn was home. How was he going to react to my turning up on the doorstep to check on his girlfriend? I decided I didn't care. I remembered how scared she'd been, dreading his reaction when he found his precious car damaged.

I knocked at the door. There was an immediate staccato yap of a small dog. I retreated from the doorstep a few paces and waited. Indoors someone shouted. Then came the thump of feet. The door cracked open a few inches.

A beefy young man in a washed-out sweatshirt glared out at me.

'What do you want?'

So this was Bryn, I assumed.

'Is Rachel in?' I asked him.

'No.' he snapped. His thick red fingers, clamped around the door edge, were inky with tattoos. He was about to slam the door shut on me.

'She wasn't at her stall today,' I said quickly. 'I said I'd call in and get some beads. I just wondered if she was OK.'

'Course she's OK. Why wouldn't she be?'

'I was with her, after the accident,' I said. 'She was quite shaken up.'

'Too bloody right!' he snapped. 'She ain't here, OK?'

'Will she be back in the market on Friday?'

'How should I know?' From somewhere indoors, the dog started yapping again. He turned and yelled at it to shut up. 'Bloody beads.' he muttered, and slammed the door.

Was Rachel really out? There'd been a handbag on the hall table. Would she have gone without it? I could hardly bang on the door again and insist I speak to her. I retreated down the path. From the roadside I stopped and looked back at the house. Just for a second I caught sight of a shadowy figure up in the bedroom window, hiding behind the curtain. Rachel? Why hadn't she come down to speak to me? Was she so terrified of Bryn? He could certainly use a few charm lessons, I thought. I headed back to my car. Friday, then. I'd go back to the market Friday. And if Rachel wasn't there, then Bryn had a few questions to answer.

5

THURSDAY

With a two-week deadline to finish the wall hanging ready for the grand opening of the Visitor Centre, I intended to spend all day sewing in my studio at Ceri Cottage. I had tried emailing Rachel the previous evening after I'd got back from Nantmawr but as yet she hadn't answered, no doubt under instruction from Bryn. I put him down as a control freak. And one who needed teaching a few lessons.

As for Gabriel, he hadn't answered my email either. I gave a sigh. So I knew we couldn't actually be together, not for a while at least, but surely we could still keep in touch, I thought crossly. I decided he must have been taking lessons from the red-haired girl in the library. Cut loose. Move on.

It was just as well I had plenty to do to take my mind off Gabriel. There was still so much surface stitching to finish, and lots of beadwork. Most of it had to be sewn by hand. I factored in the library workshops in Llannon, the school visits, the nursing homes, the talks to the WI. If I didn't bother sleeping for a few days, I should just have enough time to get it finished.

I settled at my worktable in the studio. The morning light was all but squeezed out by the rain clouds. I switched on the daylight lamp and took out the skeins of silk to work some magic into the wall hanging. I had stitched tiny scraps of pale green silk and organza among the tree trunks on the quilt, to portray the gowns of the dancing elf maidens. Now, with couched iridescent stitches of silver and green, I wanted to suggest their clasped hands, the dainty pointing feet, the tilt of their faces. It needed a lightness of touch to echo the sisters in their dance, and suggest the tinkling melody of music. And then there was Edric, glimpsed like a wolf in the darkness, watching hungrily from the shadows of the trees. As my fingers traced the shapes of the branches, I sensed a shadow at the window. I spun round, and saw a face there. It disappeared just as quickly. Then there came a loud knock at the door that set my heart racing.

'You the quilt lady?' he asked anxiously as I opened the door. He was late thirties or so, thin, his shoulders hunched in a dripping biker jacket.

'Yes. I'm Bronwen Jones,' I said, frowning. He didn't look as if he'd come for quilting lessons.

'I found your name in the library,' he said. 'She'd no right. No right at all,' he said angrily.

'No?'

'Willow just doesn't get it sometimes.' He gave a sigh of frustration.

'Willow?'

'She doesn't understand,' he said.

I was beginning to wonder where I'd acquired the Agony Aunt sign.

'I'm really sorry, but I do have some work to do,' I said gently.

'No!' He pushed the door wider open. 'Please, I've got to get them back. You do still have them?' he faltered. 'The clothes Willow gave you?'

I studied him. Rain beaded his pointy beard. With his hair scraped up in a topknot Samurai-style, his face looked thin and bony, more feral cat than warrior.

'They're in my studio,' I said. 'I'll get them for you.'

Now I pictured her: the red-haired girl, carrying that black plastic bin bag, the ice-cold expression in her eyes. No, she'd said, they weren't her things. So whose were they? Not his, surely?

'She said you were going to cut them up to make quilts,' he said, following me down the hall. 'You've not cut them up yet, have you?'

'No. The bag's there,' I told him, pointing to the bin bag by the door.

He almost fell upon the bag, diving his hands into the fabrics like a starving man at a feast.

'I promised to keep them, see? For when she comes back.' He straightened then, holding the bag in his arms, his lean face easing with a faint smile.

'Lucky you came when you did. I was going to take them into school tomorrow. You want a hand with them?' I said, suddenly anxious to be rid of him. His calm smile was more unnerving than his anxiety.

'No, thanks.'

'I'm sorry, but she, Willow, told me they weren't needed,' I explained. 'She was going to take them to the recycling.'

'She had no right!' he said fiercely. He clutched the bag more tightly against his chest. 'I told her!'

'So, they're not hers?'

'No! They belong to a friend of mine. She... she's gone away,' he said.

'How long's she been gone?'

'Almost two years now,' he said.

I stared at him, at that mild smile, the strange light of almost manic certainty in his eyes, and understood what Willow had meant. It was time he moved on. After two years, she was definitely not coming back.

6

FRIDAY

As soon as the morning workshop was over, I left the library and headed for the market. I was due to visit one of the local nursing homes that afternoon, to talk to the residents about their memories of Llannon's past. There were one or two quilters among them, the matron had told me on the phone. But if Rachel wasn't at her market stall, I intended calling at Nantmawr and Bryn was not going to stop me speaking to her.

I made my way between the stalls and saw with relief that Rachel's stall was now stocked with baskets and strings of beads. Only, as I got closer, I realised it wasn't Rachel who was standing at the stall, sipping a carton of coffee. The young woman was tall, slender, with sleek blonde hair pulled back in a ponytail. Her flawless complexion was a creamy white. She glanced up as I approached.

'I'm looking for some small iridescent beads for a quilt I'm working on,' I said. 'I asked Rachel about them. Is she here?'

She shook her head. 'She is unwell.'

From the strong eastern European accent, I guessed she was Magda, the bead-maker.

'She hasn't been here since the accident, has she?'

She stared back at me, as if she had not understood.

'The car,' I said. 'She hit a tree. I was there just after it happened.'

'I think not a tree,' she said bitterly.

'Magda, is it Bryn? Has he hurt her?' I asked.

'She is OK. Has black eye. She won't come in so she ask me. Is difficult for me. I have my baby. But I have

43

to sell my beads. I have to make money,' she said desperately. 'You say you want beads?'

'Yes. These are so pretty,' I said, peering into the little baskets of buttons and beads. There were glass beads in bright colours, some flecked with gold, others with swirls of contrast colours. All the while, I wondered just what I should do now. Report Bryn to the police? Or would that just make things more difficult for Rachel? 'These are beautiful,' I said, picking up one of the packets of small gilded beads.

'Very special. Hand-made. Each one different,' she said more eagerly. 'I have a small kiln for the glass-making.'

I made my selection, which Magda solemnly wrapped.

'When you see Rachel, tell her I was asking about her,' I said. 'Ask her if there's anything I can do. I know after the accident she was worried what Bryn would say about his car being damaged.'

'He is very angry man,' she said, her eyes lowered. 'I think she should leave him but...' She gave a shrug of her thin shoulders.

I fished my business card out of my bag and handed it to her.

'Ring me, if I can help at all.'

She studied me a moment, then slipped the card into her pocket with a nod.

I made my way back out of the market, feeling helpless. Why did Rachel stay with him when he mistreated her? Wasn't there anyone she could turn to for help? No wonder he didn't want anyone to see her. Just how long did he plan on hiding her away?

'Watch where you're going!' I snapped at the man who barged past me. I glared at him, then at his colleague. They were both dressed in black suits,

44

barrel-chested, one shaven-headed, one with close-cropped hair. Like Tweedledee and Tweedledum, I thought. The bald man glared at me as he stalked past.

I emerged into the drizzle out of doors. Parked right outside on the double yellow lines was a silver Mercedes with darkened windows. I could just imagine who it belonged to.

I glanced across the road to the newsagent's board, wondering if there was any more news on the body in the landslip. *'Police seek witnesses to hit-and-run'* ran the headline. I crossed the road and bought a copy of the local paper. In the early hours of Thursday morning, a woman had been found on the roadside, hit by a car. There was no photograph, but she was described as about twenty, with long dyed red hair. I felt a chill of horror. It had to be Willow. What had happened? My heartbeat thudded. I remembered the way the thin-faced man had looked as he stood in my studio: his fierce anger, barely suppressed, then the eerie calm of his smile. I knew they had argued over the clothes she had taken.

'What have you done?' I whispered.

The loud screech of tyres startled me. In panic I saw the silver car swoop past me, its horn blaring. I jumped back onto the pavement, my heart thumping. I wasn't aware I'd even stepped out into the road, so engrossed had I been in my thoughts. And just as the car passed, I saw her face at the window: a pale oval, her eyes wide, scared. Magda.

I ran back into the market, pushing my way through the knot of people. As I reached the stall, I saw the bustle of people, some on their knees, busily scooping up beads. Others stood round, deep in discussion. The stall had been upended. Buttons and beads were scattered everywhere, some still rolling across the tiled

45

floor. A chaos of bags and boxes. And Magda had gone. Taken by those two men, I realised.

I stared back at the doorway. What was going on? Who were these people? And where had they taken Magda?

I turned back to find the woman from the children's stall watching me warily. She gave a shake of her head.

'Don't,' she said. 'Don't interfere. Not with them.'

'But who are they?'

'You don't know them?'

I shook my head.

'Lucky you,' she said. 'I should keep it that way.'

'But they've got Magda.'

'Taken her home,' she said. 'She'll be OK.'

'But we have to do something!' I said, appalled at her calm acceptance of Magda's abduction.

'No we don't. They're Lloyd's boys. Like I say, they're just taking her home. Don't make things more difficult for her,' she warned.

'So where's "home" then?' I asked her.

'Lloyd's place. Top Farm. Fort Apache, we call it. Bandit country. You won't get within a mile without an escort.'

'She lives there?'

She gave the briefest of nods. 'Her and the kiddie. He's Lloyd's son,' she said. 'Like I said, don't interfere.'

I gave a sigh of frustration. I glanced round at the floor, now all but cleared of the scattered beads. It wasn't right. How could he behave like that, as if he were above the law? I piled the bags of beads onto the righted stall.

'Can you look after the stock till Rachel gets back?'

'I can't run two stalls,' she said. 'If Rachel wants to keep her pitch, she'll have to show up. Plenty of others in the queue, else.'

'OK. So I'll take them with me.'

Grudgingly she turned to help me pack up the rescued beads and buttons.

'Thanks,' I said when we were done. 'I'll see she gets them back.'

I made it to the Woodlands Nursing Home, a few miles south of Llannon, in time for tea and a selection of fancy cakes. Six of the elderly residents were sitting round the lounge in wheelchairs and high-backed armchairs, as if in a doctor's waiting room. From their patient smiles, I guessed that much of their lives now were reduced to waiting. I showed them some of the quilts I had brought and talked about the early days of the wool industry, when carding, spinning and weaving wool had been the work of the farms and cottages around. The fine wool from the local sheep had been sought after, and the industry had prospered. In time, there'd been bigger mills, employing hundreds. Until, inevitably, they could no longer compete with the mills of northern England, and the demand for flannel declined. By the end of the eighteenth century the boom was over. One of the women, who must have been in her nineties, said she could remember the big flannel mill in Llannon when she was a child, though even by then it was being used for processing leather.

'My mam and grandma were quilters,' one of the women told me. 'They taught me their patterns. Handed down, generation to generation.'

'Do you still have any of your quilts?' I asked her. She gave a shake of her head.

'I got rid of most of my things when I moved in here. Can't bring everything, see. There's no room.'

'We do have one lady who brought an old quilt with her,' the matron told me. She escorted me upstairs to one of the bedrooms. 'Here we are, Nell,' she announced, 'It's the quilt lady I was telling you about.'

I smiled at the frail figure lying propped up against a bank of pillows, half dozing.

'You've come to see my quilt?' she said, her pale eyes brightening. She raised a bony hand and pointed to the wardrobe. 'It's seen better days,' she said. 'Much like me,' she added with a dry chuckle.

On the top shelf of the wardrobe I found the quilt folded in a cotton sheet. Carefully I took it down and opened it out on top of her bed. It was a beautiful wholecloth quilt in pale gold cotton sateen, stuffed with soft wool, which made the intricately stitched quilting pattern all the more sculptured. The border was stitched in a traditional Welsh trail design of interweaving scrolls. In the centre was the outline of an urn with tulips, surrounded by more flower and leaf shapes, and infilled with hearts and swirls. There was hardly a space that wasn't stitched. The closely sewn patterns ensured that the wool filling would be held in place during its long years of use.

'Is this your own work?' I asked her.

She gave a nod.

'Years ago, now,' she said, her voice weak, scarcely audible. 'I made it for our marriage. It was just before the war. Sixty-six years we were together. A fine man, he was,' she said softly. I followed her glance and saw the framed photograph on the wall. A fine man, indeed, handsome in his army uniform. A second photograph showed the couple, much older, at a family celebration. I could see a cake, balloons.

'Your wedding anniversary?' I guessed.

'Golden Wedding,' she said proudly.

'You made a handsome couple,' I said.

'Two boys, we had. Tall and handsome like their Da. Good boys. Six grandchildren between them, and two great-grandchildren. They come and see me as often as they can. But they live so far away,' she said with regret.

'May I take some photographs of the quilt?' I asked her. I told her about the exhibition we were planning. 'I'd like to add the story about you making this for your wedding, and about your life together.'

She nodded, eyes drooping wearily shut.

'I could tell you some stories,' she said.

I drove away from the Woodlands, delighted I had found my first quilt for the exhibition, but for now my main concern was for Magda. I wondered if Rachel knew yet what had happened to her friend. If I couldn't phone the police, I had only one choice. I turned left at the junction in Llannon, and crossed the bridge over the river. The road headed up into the hills. Bandit country, as Carol, the stallholder, had called it. She hadn't wanted to tell me where to find Top Farm, Lloyd's house, but what harm could it do? I only wanted to return Magda's things.

A yellow metal police sign propped in the verge announced in Welsh and English that witnesses were sought for a serious accident that had occurred there between ten pm Wednesday evening and seven am, Thursday morning. The hit-and-run, I realised. Willow's accident. I slowed, saw the police tape twined in the hedgerow. I hadn't heard any more news about the accident. Was she all right?

49

The road climbed steadily along the north side of the valley. Every now and then, the dense thorn hedges parted for a gateway. I glimpsed the river now far below, rushing between its steep banks, the marshy land either side silvered with standing water. Near the top of the hill the road narrowed to a single-track lane and plunged into a belt of woodland. I just hoped I wouldn't meet anything coming towards me. I hadn't seen a passing place for some while. Then the trees gave way to a view of hills stretching to the distance like gently pleated felt. To the right, the fields were intersected by white- painted fences, not a bit like the hunkered grey stone walls of the other hill farms. Sleek horses grazed in a paddock, their glossy coats protected by chequered horse-rugs. I could see a range of outbuildings: stables, barns. The sign on the open gate said 'Top Farm'. So this was Lloyd's place.

I drove slowly up the wide gravel drive that was bordered by white fencing and immaculately clipped grass. The large windows of the long whitewashed house seemed to watch my approach. No lights showed though it was growing dark now. And I could see no silver Merc parked in the circle of gravel in front of the house. All the same, I had the feeling the house was not unoccupied. Somewhere dogs started a ferocious barking.

I swung the Land Rover into the gravel circle and pulled up next to a bronze statue in the centre of the circle: a flimsily clad woman clutching a pole between her thighs and outstretched arms. Tasteful, I thought. As I stepped from the car, security lights flicked on in a glare that momentarily blinded me. Blinking, I saw the front door open. I recognised the bald-headed man who came out onto the steps. Though he had swapped his tight black suit for jeans and a black sweatshirt, he didn't look any more relaxed. I couldn't imagine him doing 'casual'. He chewed as he came down the steps towards me. I saw he was wearing a headset with a small radio mike at his cheek.

'Is Magda at home?'

'Who wants to know?' he snarled.

'There was an accident at the market. Her stall was knocked over,' I said, careful to keep the accusation from my voice. 'I picked up most of the beads. I've brought them for her.'

He studied me a moment more, chewing all the harder, his arms folded across his barrel chest.

'Wait,' he snapped, as if to a dog.

He plodded back up the steps as he spoke to someone on the headset. I followed him, and was right behind him by the time he reached the door. From somewhere indoors I could hear the thump of music.

He turned and scowled at me. Behind him, the door opened.

'Mervyn, is there a problem?'

Mervyn stiffened.

'She's just leaving,' he muttered, glaring down at me.

'Not until I've seen Magda,' I insisted.

The door opened a fraction more. The man was short, stocky, wearing blue jeans and a pristine white polo shirt with a designer logo. And, improbably, Ray-Bans.

'I think there's been a misunderstanding,' he said, his voice light, high-pitched. 'It's all right, Merve. I'll explain to the lady.'

Merve gave a nod that was almost a bow, and sidled back into the house, his face flushed.

'Mervyn can be a tad overprotective,' the man said, taking off his sunglasses and tucking them into his

51

chest pocket. His eyes were small and chilly blue. I preferred the sunglasses. I could sense him judging me all the time, calculating what I had come for, what it would take to get rid of me. He was evidently a man used to making fast deals. 'We don't get many visitors,' he said and smiled, though with little warmth.

'I'm not surprised if that's the welcome they get,' I said. And smiled back, equally without warmth.

'So, what can I do for you, Miss...?'

'Jones. Bronwen Jones. I'm a textile artist. And a customer of Rachel and Magda's. I saw your men march off with her from the market today. Most of the stock was scattered over the floor. I've picked up what I could. It's in the car.'

'Ah,' he said. 'That was unfortunate. Eager to please, my boys, but they can be rather clumsy. It was a minor emergency. The baby was poorly, that was all. Needed his mother. He's fine now.' He turned as if to go back indoors, then glanced back. 'Oh, about the beads,' he said. 'You shouldn't have gone to all that trouble.'

I stood watching him, impotent and angry. Was he just going to dismiss me like that? Where was Magda? I didn't believe his story about the baby for one minute.

'It was no trouble. For me,' I said.

He studied me calmly, a faint smile on his narrow lips.

'You've had a wasted journey,' he said easily in that light fluting voice. 'Magda doesn't need the beads. As you can see, she has everything she wants here. She's decided not to return to the market.'

'Has she?'

He let out a breath of annoyance. He beckoned me as he walked back indoors.

'Magda!' he yelled, marching away from me.

I stood in the hall, looking round at the chocolate and gold wallpaper. A half-open door to my left revealed a bank of TV screens showing different grey images of the land around the house. CCTV, I realised. So I had been under surveillance ever since I had driven through the gateway. Mervyn's bulk loomed in the doorway. The door slammed shut. Then I noticed the life-size painting on the opposite wall: a woman much like Magda lying naked in a provocative pose. Had Magda also been the model for the bronze outside?

The thump of music ceased. A door slammed. Then I heard the tap-tap of high heels over the slate floor.

'You should not have come,' Magda said crossly when she saw me. Her face was flushed, her skin glowing. She was wearing a short black silk dressing gown with little underneath. Her glance flickered to Lloyd, as if seeking approval.

'I was just telling Ms Jones you've given up the market stall. No need for my girl to work, is there, sweetheart?'

'No,' she said, her chin tilting up.

'But your work, all those beautiful beads,' I said.

'Keep them,' she said, her glare rising to me in challenge. 'I don't want them.'

'There's your answer,' Lloyd said, patting the girl on her backside. 'See, wasted journey.' His lips drew into a broad white-toothed smile. 'I give my Magda everything she needs. Isn't that right, babe?'

'Everything,' she echoed, her face as rigid as if it had been botoxed.

There was no point in staying. I got the message. In front of him, what else could Magda say? But just the slightest tremble of her lip betrayed the emotion she was fighting to conceal. Fear, I guessed. I'd seen it in

53

her face in the back of the Merc. I backed away towards the door.

'OK,' I said. 'I'll keep the beads till I see Rachel.'

'You do that,' Lloyd said. He followed me to the door and as he closed it, his voice rasped out, any veneer of charm abandoned. 'This is my private space, my family. Don't come here again, Ms Jones.'

The slam of the door echoed across the fields.

I stood blinking in the glare of the security lights. Inside the house, all was silent. There was just one sound then: a loud, resounding slap.

I climbed back into the Land Rover, my fingers shaking as I tried to start the engine. The stallholder was right. I shouldn't have come. I'd probably made things worse for Magda now. But however had she got herself into that relationship? And, more importantly, how was she going to get out of it?

I remembered what Rachel had said. That Magda needed the money. For her and the baby. Was that it? A secret source of income, so that she could plan her escape? And now her plans were in ruins. My fault.

The car tyres skidded on the gravel as I accelerated away. That was the last time I was going to interfere. And yet, if I hadn't gone, would I have felt any more at ease?

7

SATURDAY

I woke at seven, in pitch-darkness. My first thought was Magda and her baby. I wondered how Lloyd was treating her. It seemed her relationship was little improvement on the Rachel and Bryn situation. I'd emailed Rachel the previous evening to make sure she knew what had happened to Magda and to her stall. I suggested I could drop off the stock of beads, and just hoped she'd email back this time.

I packed some of my fabric stash for the morning's workshop at the library and set off across country. Though Rachel had not replied to my email, I made sure I reached Llannon with time enough to stop by at the market.

Even at a distance I could see the bruising to her face. No wonder she hadn't been keen to show up. I pictured Bryn's red fists, heavily tattooed. How long could he go on getting away with it? Why didn't she leave him?

'I hoped you'd be in today. I emailed you,' I said. 'I've got a couple of boxes of Magda's beads in my car. Has Bryn calmed down now?'

'He's taken the Beetle over to the farm for a respray,' she said. 'I told him I'm moving out as soon as I can find somewhere.'

'Thank goodness,' I said, glad she'd come to the right decision.

'Have you heard anything from Magda?' I asked her.

'No,' she sighed. She gave a wary glance at Carol. 'I know she wants to move out, but you can see how it is. Lloyd thinks he owns her.'

'So how did she get mixed up with him?'

55

'Work,' she said. 'He owns a couple of clubs on the north coast. She was looking for work, couldn't speak the language. Ended up as a pole-dancer. Only he decided he preferred exclusive use. He brought her back here and installed her in Top Farm. Pretty soon after, she was pregnant. Now he wants another son. He's not going to let her out of his sight until he gets what he wants.'

'Is that what she wants?'

She gave me a disparaging look. 'What do you think?'

'Does she have any family or friends to go to?'

She shook her head. 'She can't even go home. Lloyd keeps her passport. She's not going anywhere without his say-so.'

'He can't do that,' I said indignantly.

'Try telling him that.'

'If there's anything I can do,' I said.

'There isn't. Believe me, if there was, we'd already have done it.'

'The beads. That's what she was saving up for, wasn't it? Her escape route?'

'To start with. Now I think she's given up.' She gave a helpless shrug. 'He'd never let her take the baby. And she won't leave without him.'

It was almost ten o'clock when I got back to the library. There was a little cluster of people waiting for me: mothers with children of various sizes. I was planning on doing some basic geometric shapes they could easily stitch together, and there were fabric pens and paints to decorate them.

Kate, the librarian, came over as I was setting up my table, a pile of audio books in her arms, her specs hanging on a chain round her neck.

'Jane, our community librarian, said a couple of her housebound customers used to be quilters,' she told me. 'Some of them have got heirloom quilts you might want to see.'

'That's great,' I said. I told her about the quilt in the nursing home. 'I'm going back next week to take some photos and write up a brief story about it. It's just the sort of thing I wanted for the exhibition.'

'Actually these are for one of Jane's ladies,' she said, glancing down at the audio books she was carrying. 'Nan Beddows. She was a keen quilter in her day. She's ordered these. They've just come in. Usually Willow would have collected them, but now, of course,' she sighed. 'It was such a shock to everyone. I don't have a phone number for Nan's grandson, otherwise I'd have asked him to collect them. Poor Peter. He must be devastated.'

'Is she badly hurt?' I asked.

'In a coma, apparently. Touch and go. Awful, isn't it? Mind, where she was going at that time of the morning, I don't know. I've not seen Peter to ask him what happened.'

I remembered what the red-haired girl had said. She was leaving, and soon. She'd been adamant about that. But had there been a row over the bag of clothes she'd brought to me? There had been no mistaking the anger in Peter's eyes when he had turned up at the cottage. What had happened? Had he taken out his rage on her? Was that why she was fleeing at that time of the morning? And just whose car had hit her?

'Look, why don't you let me take the audio books. I can deliver them to Mrs Beddows and ask her about her quilts,' I said. And one way or another I would find out exactly what had happened to Willow.

The workshop was over by twelve, and with the help of the mums and library assistants, the children were cleaned up and their bright quilt squares pinned to the board. I had another workshop that afternoon, but I would have time to drop off the books for Nan Beddows.

Following the directions Kate had given me, I drove over the bridge in the centre of Llannon, and took the left-hand road. Just after the police sign, I reached the junction which had led me on over the hilltop to Lloyd's place. There was a narrow lane leading off right, following the meander of the stream. I took the lower road on the left, which led down the valley towards the river. A narrow stone bridge spanned the river, the road turning sharply as it reached the opposite bank, climbing up through the steep meadow towards the woods that covered the higher slopes. The winding road followed the contours of the hillside and emerged at last from the woodland into another wide valley. The gentler slopes were divided into fields where sheep grazed, and, lower down the valley, a small herd of sturdy black Welsh cattle.

I caught sight of The Garth on the opposite slope of the valley. The small squat bungalow was tucked against a backdrop of trees. A patchwork of wire-netting and fencing made up a series of fields for the smallholding, where chestnut coloured hens scratched and pecked. On the bare earth beyond the house stood a polytunnel and greenhouse. I pulled into the muddy yard in front of a large shed and a ramshackle pile of old farm machinery. One of the doors of the shed was propped shut with planks. There was an air of abandonment about the place, as if it had seen better days, and no one could be bothered with repairs.

As I stepped out of the Land Rover, I felt the icy sprinkle of rain on my face. I hunched into my coat and hurried to the front porch where a pair of old boots and a cracked pot of dead geraniums stood.

'Mrs Beddows? It's Bronwen Jones. I've brought your library books.'

'Door's open,' a frail voice called.

I stepped into the dark hall. It felt scarcely warmer indoors.

I found the old lady sitting straight-backed in a rug-covered armchair beside the log-burner. She reached out and switched off the radio on the table beside her. She must have been in her late eighties. She gave me a vague smile of welcome. I could see something of Peter in her lean face. Her nose was sharp, her skin deeply wrinkled from a life spent much out of doors, her silvery hair pulled back in a no-nonsense bun, but there was a softness in her features when she smiled. She must have been very pretty when she was young, I thought.

'It was kind of you,' she said. 'Come in and sit down. Tell me what you've brought me.'

As I sat down, I noticed her gaze never quite focused on me. Of course, she couldn't see. Hence the talking books. Stupid of me not to have realised before. I wondered then how she coped in so remote a place.

The books were all romances. I read the titles to her, and the brief descriptions on the back of the cases. For each one, she gave an enthusiastic nod.

'She always picks good stories for me, dear Jane,' she said.

'Is there anything I can get you, Mrs Beddows? Can I make you a cup of tea?'

'Call me Nan. Everyone does,' she said. 'A cup of tea would be nice. I don't know when Peter will be back.'

'Peter's your grandson?'

'He's a good boy,' she said fondly. 'It was such a shock for us both to find out about Willow. Peter blames himself,' she said. 'That's where he's gone. To the hospital to see her. Poor girl, poor girl.' Her smile faded. Her brow creased with a frown. 'I thought she was happy here. We got on so well. Peter… ' She stopped herself, gave a little click of her tongue, disapproving. 'Peter shouldn't have been so cross with her.'

'He was angry with her about the clothes, wasn't he? She brought them to me for patchwork.'

'She didn't understand,' she said. 'Peter tried to explain, but she wouldn't listen. He's been every day to see her, but it's difficult. He has so much to do. The animals to feed, and me, of course. I'm no use to anyone now,' she said with a sorry shake of her head. 'I used to do all that. See to the hens, do all the cooking and mending. We were a good team,' she said. 'But my sight… they call it age-related macular degeneration. The retinas are damaged. Nothing they can do. I have a little sight just at the edges, but the central vision, the useful bit, well that's long gone. Twenty years now I've been like this. Peter never complains. He's been so good to me. And the girl… Sweet little thing, she was. We got on so well. Then one night, she just ups and goes. Didn't say a thing. Quite shook me, I can tell you. But perhaps it was too much for her after all. She was so young.'

'Willow, you mean?' I asked her, uncertain. Did she mean the other girl? The one whose clothes Willow had brought me. Two years she'd been gone.

60

'Nan? Everything all right?'

It was Peter. I hadn't heard him come in. As he came into the room, he saw me, recognised me, and I saw the suspicion in his eyes.

'Miss Jones. What are you doing here?'

'I was in the library. They had some books for your grandmother. I said I'd bring them for her.'

'That was good of you,' he said, though he didn't sound too grateful.

'How's Willow?' Nan asked him.

'Same as before,' he said, sighing.

'She'll be all right,' she soothed. 'It takes time. Time is a great healer.'

'I just wish…' he started, then thought better of it. 'Thanks. For the books,' he said gruffly, anxious for me to go.

'Miss Jones was just going to make me a cup of tea,' Nan said brightly. Visitors were few and far between, I guessed, and she was in no such hurry to be rid of me. 'We always have a cuppa this time of day, don't we?'

'Always,' he echoed with an infuriated glance at me. 'I'll see to the tea.'

'So how long has Peter lived here with you?' I asked Nan when he went out to the kitchen.

'He grew up here,' she said. 'My son, Peter's dad, went to England to look for work. He never wanted to work on the land. He met a girl there, but it never worked out. They had Peter, but then she left him. What was he to do with a child? So he brought Peter back here to live with us, and he'd send us money from time to time for his keep. Peter loves the land, loves our life here,' she confided fondly. 'Takes after his grandda. A clever boy too. He went to college, you know. Computer science, he studied. And got a good job. But when he came back here for my Jack's funeral, I could tell something wasn't right. A girl, I expect. He wouldn't say. He never did go back to his job. Lucky for me. He's worked really hard. Grows enough to feed us and a bit to sell. Takes care of all the housework and the cooking. We get by just fine,' she insisted. 'That's why I was so pleased when she came to stay. It was such a help for Peter. And he needed someone. Someone to love, and to love him. I won't be here for ever. He doesn't have much luck with women.'

Willow wasn't having much luck either, I thought. And if, when, she recovered, she wouldn't come back here to live. She'd been adamant she was leaving.

'It broke his heart when she left,' Nan said softly.

I glanced at her, puzzled. Did she mean Willow?

'A lot changed when she left,' she went on. 'He'd never been much for the television, but it was as if he wanted to turn his back on the world. No TV, no phone, no computer. He said it was to save money. We manage on my pension and what he earns from the land, but I think it was her going that changed him.'

I realised she was talking about the other girl in Peter's life. The one whose clothes he had kept. Treasured, more like, since it had been the cause of such a row between him and Willow.

'What was she called?' I asked her gently.

'Seren,' Peter said, carrying in a tray of mugs. 'Her name is Seren. It means star.'

His face was grim, unsmiling, his skin seemed all the more taut, his hair pulled back into a topknot. He glared at me as he set the tray down on the little table before the log-burner.

'Your tea, Miss Jones,' he said, handing me one of the mugs. I took it, feeling self-conscious under his gaze, aware he resented my intrusion.

'It was two years ago, wasn't it, when Seren left?' I asked.

'I didn't think she'd just take off like that,' he said. His long fingers knotted together round his mug, his nails nibbled down and none too clean.

'And now Willow. It must be very upsetting for you.'

'I thought she understood,' he said. His glance flickered anxiously at me.

I sipped my tea. I'd seen Willow alive and well on Wednesday morning, and on Thursday morning, Peter had turned up at my cottage, angry over the bag of clothes Willow had given to me. '*She had no right*' he'd said, in such a temper. And now she lay in hospital, in a coma. What had happened on the road in the early hours of Thursday morning? Where was she going? Was she running away from him?

I could hear his uneven breathing in the stillness, as if he were wrestling with something.

'I was thinking about what you said. About the quilts. Putting things to good use. The bag Willow brought you... maybe she was right. I've started to cut them up,' he said. 'Cutting them into strips. Letting go. It was quite therapeutic,' he said.

I looked at him, startled.

'You're making a quilt?'

'He says he can't sew,' Nan Beddows said, 'I told him I'd teach him,' she chuckled.

'No, not a quilt,' he said softly. 'But a rag rug, that's what I'm thinking. It would be a good use of the material, don't you think? And no sewing.'

I smiled. 'Yes, I think it would be.'

'We used to make them, years ago,' Nan said. 'Many an evening after we'd finished working. Pulling the scraps through canvas with a crochet hook. I thought maybe I could have a go now. Don't need to see for that.'

'I want to make it for Willow. For when she gets better.'

I didn't answer. I could hardly tell him that, from the way Willow had spoken, she had no intention of staying here any longer. Was that why they'd argued? Because she told him she was leaving and he couldn't accept it? Not after Seren had walked out on him. I thought of Lloyd, and the way he had acted, as if he owned Magda. Was Peter really any different?

'I wanted to ask about your quilting, Mrs Beddows,' I said. 'They told me in the library you used to quilt.'

'Oh yes, long ago, before my eyesight went.'

'Do you still have any of your quilts?' I asked.

'There's one in your room, isn't there?' Peter said.

She stiffened.

'That old thing. I don't think Miss Jones would want to see that.'

'Nonsense,' he said. 'I'll fetch it.'

'Peter, no…' she said, her thin hands reaching out to try and stop him, but too late. I heard his footsteps down the corridor. Moments later he was back, carrying the quilt over his arms.

'Made it when she was a girl. Didn't you, Nan?' he said, holding out the quilt to me.

It was single-bed size, a pieced quilt in pretty fabrics, pink, cream and soft green. But the large printed square at the centre, a vase of roses, which would have been the centrepiece of a double quilt, was cut in half and now ended on the border of the quilt.

'It's very pretty,' I said, turning it over to see the plain cream back, where the quilting pattern was more obvious. Loops and scrolls around the centrepiece, and around the wide border, an interweaving pattern of rose

64

stems and leaves, that in the two topmost corners intertwined to form a heart. Embroidered in the centre of one of the hearts was an initial 'E'.

'This quilt pattern is beautiful. And unusual. I've not seen hearts like this before.'

'That was my brother's doing,' she said stiffly. 'He used to come in after work and watch us sewing. One day he said he'd design a quilt pattern for us.'

'It's lovely. Do you know where the other half of the quilt is?'

'Other half?' she said vaguely. She reached out and stroked the fabric. With a sigh, she shook her head again. 'I can't see it,' she said. 'Can't see the pattern at all. You say there's a piece missing?'

I glanced at Peter and met his stubborn stare. If he knew where the other half was, he was not going to tell me. I wondered if he'd been the one to cut the quilt in half. It would certainly be a better fit for a single bed. Had it been damaged, or was it squirrelled away somewhere and forgotten. I thought of all the antique quilts that had ended their days in dogs' beds or covering tractors.

'If you do come across it, I'd love to see it,' I said. 'It'd be good to see the two pieces reunited.' I told them a little about the talks and workshops I was doing. 'We're having a quilt exhibition in July when the project ends. It'll be in the museum in Llannon. Quilts old and new. And there'll be a short piece telling the story of each quilt. Would you mind if I included your quilt in the display, Mrs Beddows?'

'I don't know. I don't think so,' she said. 'It's a poor old thing.'

'It's beautifully made,' I said. 'And I'm sure people would be interested to know about your brother designing the quilting pattern. Is he still alive?'

65

'No,' she said softly. 'No, he died in the war.'

'I'm sorry. But if you do change your mind about the quilt…'

She didn't answer, her gaze directed towards the logs burning in the stove. Who was she thinking of? Her long-dead brother? Of Seren, or Willow?

'Right, I'd better start back. I've got another workshop this afternoon,' I said.

'Drive carefully, Miss Jones,' he said softly.

'Thanks. And thanks for the tea,' I said, and found myself unusually eager to run out into the now drumming rain and biting wind.

8

SUNDAY

With a day free of meetings and workshops, I intended to spend the whole of Sunday working on the wall hanging for Clun Forest. It would be good to have something creative to distract me from my preoccupation with The Garth. A girl who had disappeared, another lying in hospital badly injured. The elements of the puzzle swirled round in my mind, searching for clues to what had happened. And then there was Magda's imprisonment at Top Farm. I was still incensed that Lloyd could treat her as little better than a slave. At least Rachel wasn't so much of a concern now she had decided to leave Bryn. Why had she stayed with him so long when he was violent towards her? She deserved better. Not that I was any expert where love was concerned. I had an ex-husband and a lot of bitter memories to prove it. And it wasn't exactly plain sailing where Gabriel Haywood was concerned. He'd phoned briefly, Wednesday, to assure me he couldn't wait to see me, but he had a lot to tie up before he left for the States. Obviously his career was more important to him than I was. As was his daughter. Why couldn't I just find someone more straightforward, without the whole baggage of ex-wives and spoilt, needy daughters? Maybe Vi had the best idea. I could get a dog.

As I sat stitching rows of tiny beads to the elf sisters' skirts, my thoughts slid back to Peter Beddows. I pictured him with scissors slicing up the material he had been hoarding for Seren's return. He said he had found it therapeutic. Had he really begun to find peace? Had he accepted that she was not going to come back,

67

67

or was it just a way of actively cutting her out of his life? Slicing away all she had meant to him. It seemed more like a punishment. Did he hate her for leaving him?

When the phone rang at midday, I leapt to answer it, desperately hoping it would be Gabriel. I still hadn't quite planned what tone to take with him. Too patient and understanding and I'd sound like a doormat, destined to languish on the bottom of his to-do list. But neither could I come across as too needy. I couldn't hope to compete with Lydia for his attention. I could hardly complain that he was neglecting me, since our relationship had hardly even started. No, I would need to perfect 'restrained yet passionate', to give him plenty of encouragement to come back sooner rather than later. In fact, I had so much work on over the next six months, it was probably just as well he was going away. I certainly wasn't going to be distracted by him if he was three or four thousand miles away on the other side of the Atlantic. All the same, it would be good to see him again, I thought wistfully. I could do with another of his goodbye kisses. Made me wonder how good his 'hello' would be.

'Bron, it's Rachel.'

I tried not to sound disappointed. 'Hi. How are you? Have you found somewhere else to live?'

'Me and Bryn have patched things up.'

'Oh. Well, if you're sure that's what you want,' I said, the doubt evident in my voice. She certainly hadn't looked about to forgive him last time I saw her.

'I couldn't walk out just because things got tough,' she said. 'We've been together three years now. I reckon that's got to be worth something. I just rang to let you know I spoke to Magda. She's OK. She's decided to stay with Lloyd for the time being.'

'Without any money or a passport, she doesn't really have much choice, does she?' I said.

'It's not like that. Lloyd does care about her.'

Possessive, bullying, intimidating, but caring? I didn't believe it.

'Anyway she wanted to tell you she was sorry you got caught up in things.'

'I just happened to be there when his henchmen dragged her out of the market.'

'He doesn't like her working, that's all. Not while she's got his son to take care of. And he wants another kid with her. He'll take good care of her.'

It made her sound like a brood mare.

'Well, if you're sure he can be trusted,' I said. I heard her laugh.

'Trust? Lloyd?' she said.

'I just wish I could do something to help her,' I said.

'Don't you think I haven't tried?' Rachel said bitterly. 'Don't worry, I'll keep an eye on her. She's coming over Wednesday. It's Bryn's night out with the boys.'

'Is her minder coming too?'

'Doesn't need one, does she? Where could she go? He's got her kid.' She sighed. 'Anyway, she wanted you to know she was OK. She doesn't need any help.'

'You mean Lloyd's warned her he doesn't want me turning up on his doorstep again. I've got the message.'

I hung up, feeling far from reassured about Magda's situation. Being bullied and intimidated was hardly the basis for a long and happy relationship. As Rachel had yet to understand.

Was Rachel right about not walking out just because things got tough? If three years together was worth something, how did my past history with Ed stack up? We'd been together ten years. And apart for four. I could never forgive him for his affair with Miranda. For having a child with her, and not with me. He had married her. And I was free. Only it didn't feel much of a success. Why was it so difficult to find someone to love?

I caught sight of Vi in a yellow sou'wester and anorak trudging down the lane, back from her walk with William. I waved her to come in, and put on the kettle.

Carefully she wiped the little dog's paws on the towel I kept for him by the French doors.

'If it rains much more, I'm building an ark,' she said. She shook her damp hair like a little terrier. 'How's the quilt going?'

'Slowly. At least I've got all day to work on it, and I made sure I'm not booked anywhere later in the week, just to make sure it's finished.'

'Any news of the girl in the accident?'

'Not yet. I…' She was studying me intently, waiting for me to go on. 'It's about Peter,' I explained. 'I talked to his grandmother, up at their smallholding. There was another girl, Seren, who was living with them two years ago. It was her clothes Willow brought to me to use for quilt fabric. Peter said he was keeping them for when Seren came back. Seems she upped and left in the middle of the night, just like Willow did. Only I remembered how angry Peter had been at what Willow had done. He must have been in love with Seren. I wondered if he'd tried to stop her leaving. Then when Willow walked out on him, it was just too much for him.'

Vi stared at me.

'You think he tried to stop Willow? Ran her down?'

'No!' I said quickly. 'No, I don't see how. He's only got a moped. It said in the paper she'd been hit by a car.'

'But Seren walked out too? Where did she go? Did they say?'

'No. All her stuff is still at the house. I don't know what to think. With Willow leaving in the middle of the night like that… What can have happened?'

'Not having much luck, is he?' Vi said.

'That's what his grandmother said. "*He doesn't have much luck with women.*" Willow isn't having much luck either,' I reminded her.

'How did he feel about them leaving, do you think? Was he more depressed? Or angry?'

'He was certainly angry about the clothes Willow brought me. But he was depressed, too, I'd say. Nan Beddows said it had happened before. He gave up his job to go back to The Garth. She thought it had something to do with a woman.'

'Poor thing,' Vi sighed. I glanced at her, wondering if she was about to confess her own experience of broken hearts. I had no idea if she had ever been in a relationship. She never spoke of anyone, except her sister in Bewdley, yet I couldn't believe she had always been alone. She knew all the ins and outs of my break-up with Ed. Even about the darkest times when I had come so close to kidnapping his child, but she had never revealed anything of her past to me. Perhaps there was nothing to confess, but at times I sensed a core of sadness in her, and regret. As I watched her lean down with a biscuit from her pocket to feed William, I remembered her telling me once, '*Sometimes salvation comes on four legs*'. If anyone could understand what Peter was thinking and feeling, it would be the enigmatic Vi. 'Apart from his doting grandmother, he

71

doesn't seem to have the knack of making women happy, does he?'

'He does come across as a little intense,' I told her. 'Used to his own company. But he's very committed to his gran, I can see that, and to the smallholding. It's a real alternative lifestyle. You know, no telly, no phone, no computer. From what she said, I don't think they could afford all the trappings of modern life anyway. Which is probably why Seren and Willow gave up in the end. Maybe life just got too hard.'

Vi considered this, her head cocked to one side, her eyes bright. 'I wonder if she's turned up anywhere else, this Seren.'

'She's probably found another boyfriend,' I said. 'But the thought had occurred to me. I think I'd feel a whole lot better if I knew she was safe somewhere.'

She gave a bright, determined smile.

'Let's just hope so, shall we?'

After Vi left, I found the card in my purse. On it was the phone number the young police constable had given me the day of the landslip.

PC Roberts was not available, I was told.

'DS Flint,' he introduced himself curtly when my call was transferred. I sensed he was a man in a hurry. Was I wasting police time? I glanced down at the quilt spread on my studio table, at the gauzy dancers, the wolf-like Edric watching from the shadows of the trees. Fairytales. Was I too wrapped up in my work, too remote from reality? I felt stupid. How could I ask about a missing girl I didn't know? I didn't even know exactly when she'd left The Garth. Two years, they'd said.

'I was wondering about the bones I saw in the landslip,' I said. 'PC Roberts thought they might have been a sheep, but it looked more like a human skull to me.' Was that too fanciful for the impatient and down-to-earth detective sergeant?

'We had the forensic report back,' Flint said grudgingly.

'And was it a sheep?'

'No,' he said. 'As a matter of fact, it wasn't.'

'Then, it really was a skull I saw? A human skull?' I felt strangely relieved. It hadn't been my overactive imagination after all.

'A male. Probably early twenties,' DS Flint continued. 'But the bones date back maybe seventy or eighty years.'

I did the maths. 'So, they could be pre-war then?'

'So it would seem. After this length of time it's unlikely we'll be able to identify them, but we're doing some preliminary research.'

'How… how did he die?'

'That's why we're particularly interested. He died from a blow to the skull.'

'You mean he was murdered?'

'There are a number of possibilities,' he said. 'Could have been an accident. A storm perhaps, and he was hit by a falling tree, or fell from his horse.'

'And buried?'

'It was thick woodland. He wasn't found at the time.'

'Someone's husband, or son, or brother? And they didn't find him?'

'The death is suspicious,' he agreed with audible reluctance.

'After all these years. Someone got away with murder,' I said.

'So it would seem.'

'If it hadn't been for the landslip. All that rain…'

'Thank you for your call, Miss Jones,' he said, anxious to be gone, doubtless with a pile of work on the desk in front of him, and no time to speculate over an eighty-year-old murder. I could almost hear his fingers drumming impatiently on the desktop. I glanced at the elf maidens again. They seemed to be smiling, egging me on. My stomach tightened in a knot. I swallowed hard. It felt like a betrayal, asking the question. All the same, the coincidence troubled me.

'There was just one other thing I wanted to ask,' I said.

'Mm?'

'Do you have a file of missing persons in the area, from about two years ago? Someone in Llannon said there'd been a girl who'd disappeared. Gone out one evening and never came back. She'd be about Willow's age, you know, the girl who was hit by a car last week?'

'Do you have a name for her?'

I grimaced. Sorry Peter, I thought, but I just have to know.

'Seren. She was called Seren. She was living up at The Garth at the time.'

'I'll look into it,' he said sounding frostier than ever. As if the last thing he needed was more work.

'Sorry,' I said, but he had already hung up.

I felt suddenly cold. The relief I had felt, knowing I hadn't imagined seeing a human skull in the landslip, was short-lived. What if Seren really had disappeared without trace? What if Peter had had something to do with her sudden disappearance?

I consoled myself with remembering Vi's bright smile. Seren had simply gone away, found a new boyfriend. She was safe somewhere, wasn't she?

I thought of the nursery rhyme. Spoke it aloud.

'Peter, Peter, Pumpkin eater, had a wife and couldn't keep her. He put her in a pumpkin shell and there he kept her very well.'

I wondered if Seren had ever left The Garth at all.

9

MONDAY

I had arranged to meet David Evans, the museum curator, at nine in Llannon. I parked by the library and hurried down to the half-timbered building that stood proudly in the middle of the main street. The museum was on the first floor, up beautifully carved oak stairs. The town's wool market had once been held on the open ground floor, the fleeces piled between the supporting beams. On a wet and windswept Monday morning, it was hard to imagine the bustle of the market place, the beating heart of the region's wool trade. The only noise now was from a delivery lorry parked outside the Red Lion.

David Evans was waiting at the top of the stairs, a tall, slightly stooping man in his mid-forties, with thinning hair and pale eyes behind round rimless spectacles.

'So good to see you. It's an exciting new project for us,' he said, ushering me into the museum. His prominent front teeth and the tweed waistcoat and fobwatch chain gave him the look of an Alice in Wonderland White Rabbit. As I walked into the long high-ceilinged room with its arching oak beams, I heard the click of the door lock behind me. 'Sorry,' he said, seeing the alarm in my face. 'But we're not open to the public today. Wednesday, Friday, Saturday only. At the moment. The cuts, you know.' He gave a sigh of dismay. 'Permit me to give you a guided tour, Miss Jones.'

The long room was divided by a series of display boards. Glass cases against the walls were packed with artefacts from the region's wool trade: shuttles, carding combs, sheep shears. There were old photographs of the town's mills and millworkers, who had produced the fine flannels and tweeds for which mid-Wales was famed. Posters advertised the flannels on sale, beside auction bills for farm sales, shepherds' crooks, and spindles.

'This one was taken just up the valley. Eighteen-nineties,' he said, pointing to the blown-up photograph on the wall. The black-and-white picture showed a crowd of some two hundred mill workers posed in front of a tall severe mill building. Behind them, long strips of flannel were stretched out to dry.

'On tenterhooks,' David said, close to my ear. 'I've picked out some photographs I thought you could use for the exhibition.' I could hear the faint Welsh lilt in his voice. 'The main archive is over in Newtown now. There isn't room to put it all on display here. Come on through to my office. You can tell me what you had in mind.'

The small square room at the back of the building was more of a nest than an office. With shelving all round the walls, save for a narrow window of stained glass, there was little room to move.

David slid his thin frame behind the desk, nodding to me to take the upright wooden chair opposite.

'Normally I'm here three days a week, and Thursdays I do half a day at Newtown.' He gave a toothy apologetic smile. 'I'm afraid my hours were cut a few years ago. Things haven't improved. But no matter. It gives me more time for my research. I'm writing a book,' he confided. 'A history of Llannon and the outlying villages. I hope it will prove of some use in years to come,' he said with a self-deprecating shrug.

'I'm sure it'll be very interesting,' I said.

He looked rather doubtful. 'Now, about the quilt exhibition. What have you got planned so far? I've outlined a few suggestions, here, for you,' he said, sliding an alarmingly bulky folder across the desk to me.

I gathered I was the spearhead of his campaign to have the museum open permanently for six days a week. Anything that boosted visitor numbers, and with it, the museum's income, was to be welcomed. 'I've managed to secure additional funds to open the museum for six days a week while the exhibition runs,' he told me proudly. 'It'll be the start of the school holidays and the tourist season, so I have high hopes for visitor numbers. We have to showcase all that Llannon has to offer.'

'At the moment, I'm running a series of workshops,' I said. 'I intend to display the quilts we make, and the projects the school's doing. It would be good to have some interactive displays. Perhaps someone spinning, so that people could give it a try.'

He nodded enthusiastically.

'I'm in contact with several ladies who spin and weave the wool from their own sheep. There won't be space for a loom, of course, but I think I can find a working display model.'

'Excellent. Of course we will need some more antique quilts made in the area. I've located one or two so far where the owners have agreed to loan them for the exhibition. And I'll be photographing and documenting any others we come across,' I told him.

His pale eyes gleamed at me.

'You have been busy,' he said.

'It's slow going, but there's plenty of time yet. As a matter of fact, I did find a lovely old quilt up at The

Garth. Nan Beddows made it when she was young. I'm hoping she'll agree to loan it to us.'

'You've been to The Garth?' he said, his smile faded.

'Yes. I took some audio books for her.'

'And Peter. You saw Peter? How is he?' he asked anxiously. 'I can't imagine what he must be going through. Did he say anything about her? About Willow?'

'Naturally they're both very shocked,' I said.

He nodded, steepling his long bony fingers together under his chin.

'Most distressing. It's been a great shock for us all,' he said. He studied me a moment, the light through the stained-glass window pooling in alarming shades of red and blue on his face like bruising.'I have a small private collection of flannel quilts that might be of interest to you,' he said then.

'You have?'

'I came across them as part of the research for my book,' he explained. 'I always hoped to set up a quilt museum here in Llannon, to preserve our heritage. The exhibition may well be the start of something permanent. Perhaps, if you are free one evening, you'd like to come and see the quilts for yourself.'

'I'd love to,' I told him.

He seemed to relax a little then. His smile warmed.

'That's settled then,' he said mildly.

I had a strange feeling, as he unlocked the door of the museum for me to leave, that if I hadn't agreed to his plans, he might not have been so keen to let me go.

I was due to meet Kate in the library at ten, to finalise my schedule for the week. I saw her standing at the counter when I arrived, wrapped in a shawl-collared cardigan of beige mohair. She held out the phone towards me.

'It's Peter Beddows. He says its urgent,' she told me as I approached. 'He sounds rather agitated.'

'Is everything all right?' I asked him, fearing something had happened to Nan.

'The police have turned up. They want me to go with them, but I can't... I can't leave Nan,' he said. 'I didn't know what to do, who to ask. They'll put her in a home if I'm not here.'

'It's OK,' I said, trying to sound calm, soothing. 'I can come now. I'll stay with Nan till you're back. Surely they're not arresting you, are they?'

I heard a muffled conversation, then there was another voice I recognised. DS Flint.

'If you can come, Miss Jones, it would be appreciated. We're taking Mr Beddows in for questioning. It may take a little while but we've a few things we'd like to clarify.'

'Is this about Seren?' I asked him.

'I'm sorry, Miss Jones, I'm not at liberty to say.'

He cut the call. I glanced across the library to where Kate stood, shelving books, at a discreet distance.

'I have to go,' I told her. 'I'll ring you later, if that's OK?'

I wondered if Peter realised who had tipped off the police about Seren's disappearance. There couldn't be many other suspects, could there? He'd be furious with me, I thought. Not that he sounded it on the phone. Just anxious. Or was that guilt I'd heard in his voice?

I drove through Llannon and took the road over the bridge, to the junction where the police sign still stood, asking for witnesses to Willow's accident. It couldn't have been Peter, I told myself. It hadn't been guilt in his voice, just concern for his grandmother's welfare. He was a caring person. Intense, yes, but he just wasn't the type to kill anyone. What if they did arrest him, though? If they locked him up? What would happen to Mrs Beddows then? I couldn't stay at The Garth for long.

When I reached The Garth, there was a police car and van parked beside the bungalow, and a white van from the forensics service. I could see some officers searching round the outbuildings. So they must have a search warrant, I realised. It was Seren they were looking for.

As I reached the front porch, the door was opened by a man in a dark grey suit. He looked a little like an undertaker, I thought. Close-cropped dark hair peppered with grey, and a stern unsmiling face, with dark watchful eyes.

DS Flint introduced himself. I thought how well his name suited his appearance.

'I appreciate you coming, Miss Jones,' he said, his glance swiftly appraising me. Measuring me up. Yes, a fine undertaker he'd make.

'Are you arresting Peter?'

'We need to ask him some questions. My team are making a search of the premises. It would be helpful if you could stay with Mrs Beddows and keep her calm and reassured,' he said smoothly. 'And we will have some questions for you later.'

'Of course. Though I wasn't here when Seren disappeared,' I said.

His glance was shrewd, calculating.

'No,' he said, not exactly denying that they were searching for Seren. He glanced back over his shoulder. 'Let's go.'

From the darkness of the hallway Peter came shambling out. His eyes were wide, scared, as he looked at me.

'Tell them,' he said. 'Tell them I kept Seren's things for when she comes back.'

'All right, Mr Beddows. Sooner we get there, sooner we can sort this out and bring you home.' With a nod of farewell, he marched past me with Peter and another officer, out to the car.

I found Mrs Beddows sitting by the log-burner as usual. She seemed to have shrunk since I last saw her. Her body was hunched in the chair, the rug slipped from her lap. There was a WPC sitting next to her, who got to her feet as I came into the room.

'I'll go and assist my colleagues,' she said softly.

I nodded. I knew she meant she would help with the search. I could hear them clumping about in the rooms. There was the sound of doors opening and closing, drawers being pulled out.

'Mrs Beddows, it's Bronwen. Peter asked me to sit with you till he gets back.'

'They keep asking me about Seren,' she said, her face screwed up as if in pain. 'I told them we don't know. She just left without telling us. Such a sweet girl. Peter said she was coming back, but it's been so long now. Two years.' She leaned closer to me, whispering. 'I don't think she is coming back. I couldn't say so to Peter. He was so fond of her. I think it broke his heart when she left.'

'I'm sure they'll find her soon,' I reassured her. I was glad she couldn't see the doubt in my face, but probably she could recognise it in my tone. I'd never been a good liar. 'Can I get you a cup of tea? Have you had something to eat?' I was sounding like my mother,

I realised, but in a situation like this it seemed I had to be the responsible adult.

She waved away the question.

'Peter will get my supper for me when he comes home. But a cup of tea would be nice. Oh, and ask the policemen if they'd like a hot drink, would you? They must be so cold out there.'

'Yes, of course,' I said, guilty at her kindness. Did she realise they thought Peter was a murderer?

Down the corridor I could see two officers in a bedroom doorway, deep in consultation. I headed towards them. The doors to either side were open. I saw what I guessed was Mrs Beddows' bedroom, decorated with a pale flowery paper, and a quilted chintz cover over the double bed. Was that her work too, I wondered? The room opposite was darker. In the light from a bedside lamp, I could see a single bed, a small pine chest of drawers. A plain, almost hermit-like room. Peter's, I assumed. The WPC was sitting on the edge of the bed leafing through some papers. She looked up at me, her expression stiffening.

'Tea? I'm making a pot for Mrs Beddows,' I said.

She smiled faintly. 'Thanks. Milk. No sugar.'

I reached the room at the end of the corridor where the two officers stood. My attention was caught by a large pinboard covered with photos. A pale oval face, wide dark eyes, framed by a curtain of dyed red hair. How young she looked. Younger than Willow. Was this Seren? Why were there so many photos of her?

The two policemen stopped talking and turned to me. One of them was holding what looked like a bundle of letters.

'I was going to make some tea,' I said. 'Have you found anything?'

They exchanged a wary glance.

83

'Tea would be much appreciated, Miss,' the older man said. 'Two sugars.'

He stepped forward, blocking my view into the room. I peered past him at the other officer.

'Sugar for you, too?'

He shook his head.

'No. Nothing for me, thanks.'

I wondered if they'd found the bag of Seren's clothes. I remembered then what Peter had said about cutting the fabric into strips for a rug. What would they make of his handiwork? I could just imagine them carting that away as evidence, yet it didn't mean anything, did it? I sighed. I didn't think DS Flint was the handicrafts type. Somehow I didn't think he'd understand about rag rugs.

'How much longer will this take?' I asked.

'Not much longer,' he said. 'I think we've more or less got what we need.'

'Right then. Tea for one.' I gave him a brisk smile and left them to it.

Outdoors the rain had started again. The low cloud and the woods beyond the bungalow made it seem more like dusk than midday. I pulled up the hood of my coat and hurried through the muddy yard. There was a tractor outside the larger of the sheds. A white-suited figure was bending to inspect the wheels, taking samples.

'Tea?'

He shook his head.

The double doors of the shed were slightly ajar. Inside I could see another man in a white protective suit moving about. He stooped to peer at something on the concrete floor. A uniformed officer came out, closing the door as he saw me.

'I was just about to make some tea, if you'd like some,' I said. I wondered what they were looking for, what they had found.

In the fading light it was hard to see how many others were out there in the fields, snooping round. Two? Three? In the greenhouse on the edge of the yard I could see another uniformed policeman prodding about in the pots, peering into compost sacks. Peter's moped was propped near the gate. I guessed they'd inspected it for damage, although the newspaper report had said Willow had been hit by a car.

While the large heavy kettle came to the boil on the hob, I found half a dozen chunky pottery mugs and a dainty porcelain cup and saucer I guessed was Mrs Beddows', and set them down on the formica table in the middle of the room. The small kitchen was clean, well scrubbed, the vinyl floor worn in places. The thin curtains hung lopsidedly. The room seemed to lack most of the gadgets and appliances that were modern-day must-haves. A simple pared-down existence. It had served them well for years, I supposed. Why change it? Certainly they didn't have the money to change it. And, I realised, there was an order to everything. Tea caddy. Sugar bowl. Teapot. Everything lined up precisely, so that an elderly lady with little sight could find her way round and come to no harm.

'Miss Jones?'

I swung round. It was the younger police officer.

'Changed your mind about the tea?' I asked him.

'No. More of a latte man, myself,' he said. 'No, the boss has been on. He wants us to ask Mrs Beddows a few more questions while the grandson isn't here. And he thought it might be a good idea for you to be on hand. Just to reassure her.'

'Of course,' I said, doubtful that they'd get anything more out of the old lady. She plainly didn't know anything more about Seren's disappearance. 'Just let me take these out to your colleagues.'

'I can do that,' he said easily, gathering up the mugs and putting them onto the tray I'd found. He nodded towards the window and the large vegetable garden beyond the greenhouse: neat rows of sprout plants and cabbages, netted over, an expanse of bare earth liberally mulched with manure. 'Keen gardener, Mr Beddows.'

'It's their livelihood,' I said.

'All that digging,' he mused.

I felt my face heat. 'You think he killed her and buried her out there, don't you?' I said crossly.

He looked back at me, a faint smile on his lips.

'Don't you?'

I carried the rest of the mugs up the corridor, then took Mrs Beddows her tea. In the hall there were two boxes of documents and, of course, the bag of clothes Peter had been cutting up. The WPC came out of the far bedroom carrying a folder.

'The fabric,' I said. 'Peter told me he was cutting it up to make a rug.'

'Oh?' she said, and nodded. 'Thanks for the tea.' I could tell she didn't believe me.

As I sat down again beside Mrs Beddows, I was aware of the older police officer watching us from the doorway.

'We're about finished, thank you, Mrs Beddows. I hope it hasn't been too much of an inconvenience for you.'

She didn't respond. She sat very still. It was as if she were holding her breath, willing them to go, to leave her in peace. She looked up suddenly, turning her head in the direction of the doorway.

'When will my grandson be back?'

'I can't say, at the moment,' he said. 'I hope it won't be too long. There are just a couple more questions, if you don't mind?'

She let out a vexed breath.

'Oh, very well. But there really is nothing else I can tell you.'

'You've been very helpful,' he said patiently, padding into the room. He was tall, long-legged, and bowed his head as he moved as if he were used to low-beamed cottages, wary of bumping his head. He got out his notebook and leafed through the pages. Carefully he lowered himself onto the small chair on the other side of the log-burner, his knees bending up close to his chest. 'Do you remember where Seren came from?'

'I told you. There was a folk festival in the town. When the others left, she stayed. She came to ask for work. Peter said she could stay and help on the land, in return for her bed and board. She was very young. I think she just needed somewhere safe for a while.'

'And you don't know her full name?'

'No.'

'Or her age?'

'No. I told you already. And as I can't see faces, I could only judge by her voice, by what she said. She sounded very young.'

'According to your grandson, she was sixteen,' he said.

'Was?' Her head jerked up, her gaze searching for him.

'Two years ago,' he said. 'So now she's eighteen or nineteen. Young women change a lot in that time. We've taken a few of the photos from the board, but I doubt she'll look the same now. And without her full name, it's going to be hard to trace her,' he explained.

'So if there is anything else you can remember that will help us find her, any little detail...? She must have family somewhere.'

I remembered the bundle of letters he had been holding in the bedroom. Where had they come from?

'She never spoke of them,' Nan said. 'I always had the feeling she was running away from something. At least here, she found peace for a while.'

'And she was with you for just over a year, you said?'

'Yes. A year. Then early one morning she'd gone. Not a word to either of us.'

'She hadn't told Peter she was leaving? Didn't thank you for letting her stay here all that time?'

She shrugged.

'I don't think she was ungrateful,' she said. 'And if she couldn't face saying goodbye, then I couldn't blame her for that. I just hope she found somewhere safe. A real home.'

'It didn't worry you, then? A young girl like that, on her own in the world?'

'Of course. But that's their way of life these days. Always travelling. She talked of going to Thailand. That's what we thought. She must have hitched a ride with someone.'

'But she never got in touch again?'

'I told you.'

'Yet your grandson kept all her things. Her clothes. Her photographs. Didn't you think it strange that she didn't take anything with her when she left?'

'I don't know what she did or didn't take,' she said crossly. 'I can't see, can I?'

'No. I'm sorry,' he said contritely. 'And no one ever came here asking about her?'

'No. I told you.'

'You don't have a phone in the house, Mrs Beddows?'

'Can't afford one.'

'Must make things difficult.'

'What things?'

'Keeping in touch. Getting help if Peter's out. He does go out, doesn't he?'

'He has his rounds. The vegetables, the eggs. Market once a week. We get by.'

'But you used to have a phone? There's a socket in the hall.'

'It costs too much,' she said crisply. 'Besides, who'd want to ring us? People know where we are if they want to come and talk to us. I never go out.'

'Whose idea was it to get rid of the phone?'

'Peter's. He handles the money. He got rid of it, and the computer. Said we could manage without, and we do. Don't need a TV, do I? I have my radio.'

'So, when was that? When did he get rid of the phone?'

'Two years ago. After Seren left. Only the other day he was telling me how much we'd saved.'

'So it would be hard for her to get in touch and tell you where she was,' he commented.

'She could have written if she wanted. Sent us a postcard from Thailand.'

'And did she?'

'I wouldn't know. Peter didn't say she had.'

He flipped his notebook shut and got slowly to his feet, stretching to ease his back.

'Thank you, Mrs Beddows. I'm sure we'll get this all cleared up shortly.'

She turned her head, following his direction as he moved towards the door.

'Peter said she'd come back,' she told him. 'I never believed him.'

'No?'

'I think that's why she went when she did. In the early morning before we were up. He'd have tried to stop her else. He worshipped her.'

'And how did she feel about that?'

She gave a sad smile.

'She was sixteen. Peter's twice her age. What do you think?'

I gathered up the empty mugs after the police had gone. I couldn't help but go down the corridor to the room where I'd seen the pinboard. '*Worshipped*,' Nan had said. That's what the room looked like: a shrine. The board had been covered with pictures of Seren. Some gaps now where the police had removed them, doubtless to spread information about her disappearance. A string of her beads and a tie-dyed scarf were draped round the board. A small grey teddy bear, a hand-painted pottery mug, a fabric elephant, a dish of Indian bracelets were still lined up on the bookshelf where she had left them. And all her clothes still in the drawers and the narrow wardrobe, until at last, in exasperation, Willow had pushed them all into a rubbish bag and brought them to me.

The single bed was covered with a bright patchwork. Patterned squares surrounding a large central star made up from triangles. Hadn't Peter said her name meant 'star'? I wondered if she had made it during her stay. Nan would have enjoyed that, encouraging her. I remembered the bed in Peter's room was a single, too. So had both Seren and Willow slept apart from Peter? What kind of relationship had they had?

'She'll miss him. Willow will know he hasn't come to see her today,' Mrs Beddows fretted as I came back from washing the mugs in the kitchen.

'I'll ring the hospital and let them know he'll be in as soon as he can,' I said, taking out my mobile phone.

'Would you?' She looked exhausted. 'Poor Peter. I just wish he had someone to settle down with. Do you have someone, Miss Jones?'

I hesitated. I hoped she wasn't trying to matchmake.

'Not now. I'm divorced,' I said.

'Do you have any children?'

'No. No, we'd decided not to start a family until we got the business up and running, but then Ed went and had an affair with one of our clients. She was younger, prettier.' And thinner, I could have added. Miranda had that effortless glamour and elegance I'd never come near to. 'They have a child. She's four now.'

'Couldn't you patch things up?'

'I think we've moved on too far for that,' I said.

She sighed.

'Willow always wanted Peter to move on, to forget about Seren. She didn't understand how much he'd suffered when she left him.'

'And then Willow decided to move on, too,' I said gently.

'He was afraid she would. But there was nothing he could do to stop her.'

Except by killing her, I thought.

After I phoned the hospital and left a message about Peter, I sat with Nan Beddows for a while as she listened to the radio. By and by her head drooped and she began to snore gently. I went back into the kitchen, feeling hungry. There didn't seem a great deal to eat apart from eggs so I decided to make scrambled eggs and toast. Mrs Beddows would have to be persuaded to

91

eat; there was a chance Peter wouldn't be back until morning.

She ate, unwillingly, fretting all the while that her grandson should be there, that they wouldn't feed him. She would rather have waited for him to come home. I washed the dishes, then helped her to her room to get ready for bed.

'He may be late,' I said. 'But I'll be here until he comes back.'

At last she was settled into her bed, her radio beside her playing softly. I brought her a drink of warm milk and the biscuit she asked for.

'I hope you don't think I've been ungrateful,' she said.

'Not at all. I know you're worried about Peter, but there's no need. He'll soon be back home, I'm sure.'

She gave me a grateful smile, though whether she believed me or not it was impossible to say.

'Is there anything else I can get you? Anything I can do?'

'There's the hens,' she said, suddenly remembering. 'Check on the water and feed, and shut the hens in for the night. That was always Willow's job except... Except when Peter did it,' she corrected herself. I glanced at her in suspicion, wondering what she had been about to say.

'I'll go and make sure they're OK. Can't have the foxes getting into the hen house while he's away.'

I pulled on my coat and went out through the kitchen into the yard, grabbing the large torch which hung by the back door. Outside, a security light flicked on, reflections glinting in the puddles. The rain had stopped now, but the wind still gusted from the woods. I could hear the creak and rustle of branches, like ships' sails and rigging. In the field, water glinted in the ploughed channels. A great deal of soil to dig. So many places to hide a body.

I shivered, the wind tugging at my hair, stinging my face. Across the yard I saw the tractor and Peter's moped. Behind them stood the shed with the double doors. I wondered just what the police had found so interesting in there.

I picked my way through the puddles and opened the door, shining my torch round the interior. The floor was scattered with straw. Bales were piled in the corner. And behind them, the torchlight glinted on a mirror. I went further into the shed. There it was, half hidden by the straw bales, an ancient mud-caked Land Rover.

I let out a gasp. That was what had attracted the forensic officer's attention. He wanted to know if the vehicle had been used recently.

I pushed aside the topmost bale beside the Land Rover and crouched down to inspect the metal body, tracing my fingers over the mud-encrusted bumpers, seeking any telltale dents.

'You think it was me?'

Peter's voice startled me. I lost my balance, sprawling back on the straw, the torch beam strafing wildly over the shed roof.

'When did you get back?' I said, breathless, getting to my feet.

'They just dropped me off,' he said. He stared at me, arms folded across his chest. 'You think I tried to kill her, too?'

'I saw them in here earlier. I just wondered what they'd been looking at,' I said. 'Is it yours?'

He shook his head.

'Belonged to my grandfather.'

'Still goes?'

'Can't afford to run it,' he said almost sneering.

'Then they'll be able to tell it hasn't been driven in a while.'

'Didn't say that. There's emergencies,' he said. 'Keep some red diesel for the tractor, don't I? They'll prosecute for that if they can't find anything else.'

Would they find anything else? I shivered again. He looked angry. I could sense the bitterness and rage coiled up tight inside him. It wouldn't take much for him to lash out.

'I came to shut the hens in for the night,' I said, making a move towards the door.

'I can do that. Don't need your help. You've done quite enough,' he said, his dark eyes glaring. So he knew I'd told the police about Seren's disappearance.

He turned and strode out, back across the yard to the kitchen door.

'Peter, wait, please!' I ran after him. 'What choice did I have?'

'There's always a choice,' he spat back.

'You said yourself you don't know where Seren went, what happened to her. What if someone tried to hurt her, like they hurt Willow? I couldn't bear to say nothing.'

He stopped, his hand on the door.

'Seren's all right. She can take care of herself.'

'You don't know that.'

I saw his fingers clench and unclench. He glared back at me.

'I didn't kill her.'

'I know that.'

'Do you?' He gave a slow nod. 'You'd better go. I'll tell Nan you said goodbye.'

'Peter!' I called out, but he had slammed the door. Moments later the lights were switched off and I was alone in the darkness of the yard.

10

TUESDAY

I seemed hardly to have slept before the alarm sounded. At least the morning was dry, though it was still dark. It seemed far too early to be doing anything sensible. But I had a schedule, and even now I envisaged households all over Llannon waking up, heading out onto the cold dark streets, converging on the library where I'd arranged a patchwork workshop for children. I hated school holidays. Hated shops full of other people's children and grandchildren barging about, shrieking, tugging shopping trolleys in my way.

But the library, when I arrived, looked as serene as always. Lianne, the children's librarian, had pushed back some of the shelves and had set up two tables for us to work on. The bookshelves displayed a tempting range of textile-related books: copies of *The Velveteen Rabbit*, *Elmer, the Patchwork Elephant*, *Calico Cat, Patchwork Dog*, and Beatrix Potter's *Tailor of Gloucester*, and stories of wool and spinning, from beautifully illustrated nursery rhyme *Baa Baa Black Sheep* books, to fairy tales like *The Sleeping Beauty* and *Rumpelstiltskin*. I almost wished I could spend my morning drooling over the pictures. I might be no good with children, but I loved their books.

I lugged in my sewing machine and set it up on the far table.

'All ready for battle?' Kate asked, bringing me a coffee.

I grimaced.

'How many are coming, do you think?'

'We've twenty on the list. Don't look so scared. You'll be fine. Lianne's here for moral support. She's doing the storytelling after you've finished.'

I set out pots of paint and some simple stencils I'd made out of foam. I arranged the coloured squares of fabric I'd cut, making a rainbow across the bigger table. By ten o'clock, I had a little array of eager-eyed children sitting cross-legged on the floor cushions before me.

It went more smoothly than I'd feared. We'd handed out plastic aprons and plenty of kitchen roll. Lianne proved an expert in stemming the tide of spilt paint before it hit the floor. The stamping and stencilling produced only a few squabbles over who wanted the sheep shape next. And why was there no dog? Of course, coming from sheep farms, they'd be used to having sheepdogs around. As the squares were painted, and little fingers carefully wrote their names in fabric ink, I gathered them up and began to sew the pieces together. The result was a bold, colourful spread of lollipop trees, sheep and rectangular houses with triangular roofs: a child's eye view of their local landscape. Lianne helped me to pin it across the wall above the bookshelves so that the children could see their handiwork. I had to admit, it did look cute.

I packed away the paints and cleaned up the table-top while Lianne started to read one of the books to the little crowd. I went into the cupboard that served as a kitchen, and made another coffee.

'How did the meeting with David go?' Kate asked me.

'We made a good start on the exhibition layout,' I said. 'David's got a few ideas of his own.' I remembered the thick file he'd given me, and which I hadn't yet had time to read through.

'I'll bet he has!' she grinned. 'He does take things very seriously.'

'He's really keen to get the museum open all week again. Can't blame him, I suppose.'

'The exhibition will certainly boost tourist numbers.'

'I told him I'd only got a few heirloom quilts lined up so far. He says he's got a few of his own I can take a look at.'

'Don't worry. Before you know it, you'll be swamped with quilts. Word is getting round,' she reassured me. I knew that the librarian on the library bus that went out every day to the surrounding farms and villages was doing all she could to coax and nag people into searching their lofts and outbuildings for old quilts. I thought of Mrs Beddows' beautiful half-quilt with the rose heart design. Such a shame she couldn't find its long lost partner.

'Better news about that girl, the hit-and-run,' Kate said.

'Willow? She's OK?'

'Conscious,' she said. 'One of our readers has a daughter who's a nurse in the hospital.'

'Has she been able to remember what happened?'

She shook her head.

'Not yet. Memory comes back bit by bit. Though sometimes it never fully recovers.'

'She's going to be all right, though?'

'They think so. Physically she's just got a broken arm, but that'll mend.'

'It'll be a relief to find out what really happened,' I said. A relief for Peter, I was sure. And yet the Land Rover, hidden in the shed, was a worry. It had been used recently. I guessed that from the way the forensics officer had been intently inspecting the tracks on the concrete floor. But surely Peter hadn't done anything foolish in a fit of temper?

'So where are you off to this afternoon?'

'Another of the nursing homes on the list,' I said. 'And this evening I've got a WI talk.' I really needed to get home and finish the wall hanging; it was so tantalisingly close to being ready. If I could just have one more clear day at it.

As I left the library and stowed my bag and sewing machine in the back of my Land Rover, I caught sight of a couple with a buggy across the street. There was something familiar about them. And then I recognised Magda, looking radiant in a cream fur hat and a long tan leather coat over her high tan boots. And beside her, as if riding shotgun, was her minder, Mervyn. I hesitated. Should I ask how she was? I know she'd tried to warn me to keep my distance, but what harm could it do? I waited for a gap in the traffic. Magda had stopped outside the chemist's. She parked the buggy and went inside. Mervyn stayed on guard on the pavement next to the buggy. He stooped down, reached out a fat forefinger and tweaked back the cover from the buggy. I could see him grinning. As I hurried across the road to them, I could hear him softly singing.

'*The wheels on the bus go round and round…*'

He hadn't seen me. I pushed open the door of the chemist's and went in. Magda was wandering down the aisle of baby paraphernalia, an alien world to me, of pastel colours with here and there a vivid splash of gaudy plastic.

'Hi,' I said, almost in a whisper, though Mervyn couldn't hear us. 'How are you? Is everything OK?'

She looked startled. She had selected some jars of baby food from the shelf and now stood weighing them in her hands. Her glance went anxiously to the shop window where Mervyn was still stooped talking to the child.

'It's OK,' I told her quickly. 'He didn't see me come in.'

'We're fine,' she said stiffly, though her eyes told a different story. 'Please, you must understand how it is. Lloyd, he does love me very much. And the baby. He would not hurt me or his son.'

I nodded, not believing her. I had heard that resounding slap, hadn't I, after the door had closed on me.

'I spoke to Rachel. She said there was nothing we could do to help you. But…'

'Nothing,' she cut in. 'I can handle Lloyd. Please, you must not worry. You must not come to the house again. Lloyd would be angry.'

And yet she'd been the one working, desperate to sell her beads, so she could save some money of her own to escape. What had changed? Had she simply resigned herself to her fate as Lloyd's property? At least Rachel still had the choice, though even she had relented, and stayed with Bryn. I wasn't sure that was a wise decision.

'Rachel told me she and Bryn have made it up now. She'd been about to leave him.'

'I think she should go. He is no good for her,' Magda said, tilting up her chin with a look of defiance. 'I told her so. She thinks she can change him, but it is too late.'

I sighed. From the little I'd seen of Bryn, I had to agree with her, but then I was no expert where men were concerned.

'You heard about Willow? The girl that was in the hit-and-run? Turns out she's going to be OK. She's out of the coma now.'

'She is?' Her glance darted back to the window. Mervyn had straightened up. He was looking up and down the street. She gave me a quick anxious glance, bundled the jars into my arms. 'I have to go. Don't come after me,' she said, and almost ran from the shop.

Mervyn looked up as she emerged, his smile swiftly turning into concern. I could see her talking quickly, shaking her head. Yes, she was fine. They didn't have what she wanted. She walked on hurriedly up the street with Mervyn following in her wake pushing the buggy. He looked back, once, glancing at the shop window in bewilderment. I ducked back out of sight, hoping he hadn't seen me. The last thing I wanted was to make things more difficult for Magda.

'Can I help?'

I turned to the woman in the white jacket.

'She changed her mind,' I said with an apologetic shrug, handing the jars back to her.

Across the street was the Daisy Chain café. It was busy now with lunchtime shoppers. I squeezed behind a small table at the back of the shop and gave my order to the young girl who was waitressing. Curried carrot soup, and redbush tea. Soup always made me feel virtuous, every spoonful packed with vitamins. It didn't feel so bad then, ordering the chocolate fudge cake.

I watched the girl retreat to the kitchen with my order. She looked school-age, long dyed black hair in a ponytail. Under her navy apron she wore a tight-fitting black-and-cream striped jersey top that made her long thin arms look puppet-like. With her white makeup and dark lipstick, she reminded me of Caitlin, the girl I'd tried to help last summer when she'd been intent on

100

running away from home to go travelling. Not unlike Seren, I thought. I wondered if Seren had come in here for food. Would they remember her? Maybe she'd even come here to meet friends. She had to have friends her own age, didn't she? Mrs Beddows was right. Peter would be twice the girl's age. How much would they have had in common? But the young waitress would still have been at school two years ago. As she brought me my soup, I took the chance to ask her.

'I was wondering if you knew a friend of mine. She was living here until about two years ago. Seren, she was called.'

'Sorry,' she said with a warm smile that seemed quite at odds with her severe Goth image. 'Maybe Rhiannon would know. She's the boss. Why don't you ask her?'

I saw the older woman behind the counter. She was busy serving an elderly couple who had just come in and couldn't decide which cakes to choose. When there was a pause in serving customers, the waitress went across to her and pointed me out. I saw the woman frown, shake her head. Then with a glance round the room to make sure all her customers were attended to, she emerged from behind the counter and stood before me, arms folded.

'You were asking about Seren?' she said.

The woman was around my own age, I guessed. No wedding ring. Her dark curly hair was pulled back in a band. She wore tight jeans and a baggy navy sweatshirt under an apron stencilled with a ring of daisies, the café's logo.

'I thought she might have come here. To meet friends perhaps. She was living up at The Garth for a while.'

'With Peter. Yes, I knew her,' she said evenly, her dark eyes narrowed with suspicion. 'You said you were a friend of hers?'

I gave an apologetic smile.

'I lied. I didn't know her at all. I just wondered where she'd gone, that's all.'

She nodded, accepting I was telling the truth, and eased herself down onto the chair opposite me.

'I heard the police had been up there, searching his place. They think he did her in,' she said grimly. 'I could tell them. Peter wouldn't hurt a fly.'

'So you know Peter?'

'Of course. Who doesn't? He supplies eggs and veg for us. Salads in the summer. Good local produce, that's what we want. And we know it's all organic. You can trust Peter for that.'

'So he comes in here regularly?'

'Once a week, yes. Sometimes I drive up there and collect if it's a big order. Nan likes the company, too. They don't get too many visitors up there.'

'You remember Seren?'

'Yes. Quiet little thing, she was, but always a sunny smile. Always ready to help. She helped out weekends in the summer when we were busy. Most times she worked with Peter up at The Garth.'

'Did you have any idea she was planning on leaving so suddenly?'

'No,' she said, but there was doubt in her voice. 'You can never tell when they're that age. I've a daughter myself. She's off travelling round India. I'd rather she didn't, of course, but I can hardly stop her when I did exactly the same thing myself.' She gave a brief smile. 'Doesn't stop you worrying though, does it? I mean, remembering what I used to get up to at their age. You got kids?'

'No. Too late now,' I said.

'Well, at least you can sleep at nights,' she said.

'But Seren, did she say anything about what she was planning?'

'Peter asked me. He was really cut up about it when she'd gone. He and I, well, we fell out. I think he suspected I'd helped her. She must have been saving up the money she earned here, then one day, that was it. The wind changed, or whatever, and she was gone.'

'Did you worry about her, too?'

'How do you mean?'

'That maybe something had happened to her?'

There was the scraping of chairs. A couple with a small child had finished their lunch and were making ready to leave. They approached the counter with their bill, looking round for Rhiannon. She got to her feet, put on her smile and chattered to them in Welsh. They paid for their lunch, strapped the child back into the buggy they'd left by the door, and Rhiannon held the door open for them, watching them safely off the premises. Only then did she return to me. This time she didn't sit down. She leaned on the table, her head close to mine.

'Don't go stirring things up for Peter. He's had enough to cope with. You won't do him any favours.'

'Even if I find Seren?' I insisted.

'Maybe she doesn't want to be found.'

'Had they fallen out, her and Peter? Did he try to stop her leaving?'

'He wasn't the one she was running away from,' she said.

'Then who?'

'Ask Peter,' she responded. 'Now, chocolate fudge cake, wasn't it?' she said breezily, returning to the counter. 'Anwen, can you clear the far table please.'

On my drive across country to visit High Banks residential home, I kept going over in my mind all that Rhiannon had told me. Which wasn't a lot. Except there was some mystery about Seren, some reason she wanted to stay hidden. Yet Rhiannon insisted it hadn't anything to do with Peter.

'*Wouldn't hurt a fly,*' she'd said. Yet I'd been aware of the anger suppressed in him. How well did she really know him?

And then there was Magda. Though she hadn't exactly been overjoyed to see me, at least she had spoken to me. Until the moment I had told her about Willow regaining consciousness. Why would that have alarmed her? What was she afraid of Willow remembering? I could only think of the way the silver Merc had swept up the street that day, almost running me over. If I hadn't stepped back onto the pavement in time, it would have hit me. Were they hoping to keep Willow quiet, hoping she wouldn't remember? There was only one person I could ask about how Willow was. All the answers, it seemed, depended on Peter. And he was the one person I couldn't ask. He'd made it plain he didn't want to see me back at The Garth again. And yet, I could hardly give up, could I? Whatever he knew, I was sure he must have told Nan Beddows. It was just a matter of finding the right question. And I did have a reason to go back to talk to her. I still wanted one of her quilts for the exhibition. Wasn't that reason enough to go back there? And even if I couldn't persuade her to lend one of her quilts for the exhibition, I could try and prompt her memory about Seren's mysterious past, and maybe find out how Willow was, if she had remembered anything yet. At least if Peter was out delivering eggs once a week, or visiting the hospital, I'd have a chance to visit The Garth then. It was just a question of knowing when he was out.

After my talk about the town's textile heritage and the traditions of patchwork and quilting in the area, I sat impatiently with the Home's residents, drinking tea and eating custard creams, awaiting my chance to phone the Daisy Chain café and ask what day Peter delivered to them.

As soon as I piled my bags into the Land Rover, I got out my phone.

I thought for a moment that Rhiannon was not going to tell me. I could sense the hostility in her voice. She didn't trust me. She was protecting Peter, I knew. But why did she think he needed protecting? Couldn't she see that I was only trying to help? By finding Seren, I'd be able to clear all suspicion from Peter's name.

'He comes in Wednesday mornings,' she said. 'Tell him you called, shall I?'

'I'd rather you didn't,' I said.

'No. Thought not,' she said icily, and cut the call.

Now I felt really guilty, as if I were deceiving him. But if he wasn't willing to let me help him, what choice did I have?

Wednesday morning. Tomorrow. It didn't give me long to fit in a visit to The Garth. I had planned to be in the library all morning, a drop-in session, working on some quilting pieces so that people could come along and try it for themselves or hopefully remember quilts they'd got stashed away somewhere at home. Depending on what time Peter delivered to the café, I should just have time to drive up to The Garth and see Mrs Beddows.

I drove back into Llannon. There wasn't time to go back to Bishop's Castle to change, have something to eat, and drive back again to set up for my talk to the village WI. I parked at the back of the Red Lion and studied the menu chalked on the board outside. Good hearty food. I felt ravenous; it seemed an age since lunch.

I was one of the first customers that early in the evening. I chose a table near the blazing log fire and sipped a fruit juice and lemonade. I'd have preferred a chilled white wine, but I needed to be fully alert to tackle the winding lanes in the hills around the little town. I just hoped I wouldn't hit any more landslips.

I picked up a copy of the local paper someone had left and flicked through it while I waited for my sausage and mash to arrive. At the bottom of one of the pages was a short paragraph headed '*Mystery of bones find*'. My landslip man, I realised. He must have been a local man, surely. The newspaper article was intended to jog a few memories, seeking clues into a disappearance long forgotten. I wondered if someone was sleeping a little less easily in their bed. After all these years, they must have thought they had got away with it. Of course, after all this time, they were more than likely dust and bones themselves. No wonder DS Flint wasn't keen to pursue it. All the same, it was intriguing. I wondered if there were any newspaper articles from years ago citing the disappearance of someone, asking for witnesses, in the way Willow's accident had been advertised by a board at the side of the road. Of course, with no exact date to look for, it would take ages to trawl through all the newspapers for maybe a decade, and even then there might be no mention of it at all. I wondered if David Evans at the museum might take on that task. Someone had to know who the body was. It had been someone's

106

son, as I'd said to DS Flint. Someone's husband or brother. You couldn't just disappear like that. And yet, I realised with a shiver that the fire's heat did nothing to soothe, Seren had done exactly that. What had she been running away from?

The evening's talk with the WI was a delight. Not only were most of the women in the audience keen needlewomen, but several volunteered to bring me heirloom quilts they'd been given by their mothers and grandmothers. I would have plenty to display at the exhibition, and someone to help me photograph and catalogue them. David's hopes of a permanent exhibition at the museum were a step closer to being realised. I wondered if I should ring and tell him, and at the same time ask about the newspaper archives. He would be best placed to go digging out information about missing people. And I was curious to see the traditional flannel quilts he had collected.

Back home at Ceri Cottage, I poured myself a large glass of Sauvignon Blanc and put my feet up on the sofa. Bliss. I topped up the glass, found some peanuts in the cupboard. Tomorrow I would go back to The Garth and do my utmost to find out exactly what Mrs Beddows knew about Seren. I wondered if Willow had spoken to the police yet; I was sure they'd be waiting at her bedside. It would solve so much if she could just remember what had happened. Amnesia was always a potential problem, Rhiannon had said. And someone had good reason to want her memory to fail her.

My phone rang, startling me awake.

'Bronwen? It's David. David Evans,' he said hesitantly. 'I hope you'll forgive me ringing this late. I did try earlier but there was no answer.'

'No. I was giving a talk to the WI,' I said. 'I think we should have a few more heirloom quilts for the exhibition.'

'Splendid. That's partly why I was ringing. I wondered if you'd care to come over and look at my little collection. I could make Thursday evening, if that would be convenient?'

I smiled. He could only be a couple of years older than me, but there was something decidedly antique in the way he spoke. Must be the result of spending all his time in the past.

'Thursday would be fine,' I said.

'I'm in Llannon. I've got one of the old weavers' houses by the river,' he said. 'River Walk, number three. If you'd care to come for about six, I can make a light supper for us. We can go through my ideas for the exhibition. I'm really interested to hear what you made of my ideas in the little folder.'

'Of course. Delighted,' I said, my heart sinking. I had the quilt to finish for Friday afternoon. I wasn't going to have time to study his 'little folder' before then. 'There was something I was going to ask you. About your research,' I said. 'You'll have heard about the body they found in the landslip.'

'Indeed yes. Most curious,' he said.

'That's just it. I wondered if there had been any report in the newspapers of the time. I know it's going back a long way so there probably aren't any records now.'

'We do have the local papers on microfiche at Newtown,' he said.

'Do you think there'd have been anything about a young man going missing? An appeal for witnesses?' I said.

He was silent for a moment. I guessed he was trying to work out how to phrase a polite refusal to help.

'I'll be in Newtown on Thursday. I'll see what I can unearth,' he said. I wasn't sure if it was meant as a joke. 'I'll see you at six and report back on my findings.'

11

WEDNESDAY

I reached Llannon before the library opened. I took the time to wander down the street past the Daisy Chain café and checked in at the window. No sign of Peter. I wondered what time he'd come to deliver the eggs. In the market I found Rachel busy setting out baskets of beads and buttons. She didn't exactly look thrilled to see me. Her dark spiky hair seemed to bristle as she caught sight of me. The bruising round her eye was shaded between violet and ochre. She looked as if she hadn't slept in days.

'How are things with you and Bryn?' I asked her.

She pushed an empty box under the stall, straightened, and rubbed her hand over her forehead as if to ease away a headache.

'I don't know. Don't know if I'm doing the right thing. Magda said I was a fool.'

'She's in no position to lecture anyone, is she?' I said gently. 'Want me to get you a coffee?'

She gave a weary smile. 'Thanks. Make it a strong one.'

By the time I returned she was negotiating a sale with an elderly lady almost submerged in a padded anorak. She bought four buttons. Rachel counted them out carefully into a paper bag and took her money.

'I think I might go away for a few days,' she said, sipping the coffee gratefully. 'It'll give me time to think. Me and Bryn had another row. I'd planned to see Magda this evening but now she can't come.'

'Lloyd won't let her out?'

'Something like that,' she said helplessly. 'So I asked Bryn, why don't we have a night in together, get a pizza, a DVD, just the two of us. But he refused. Wednesday is boys' night out, see. I told him we couldn't afford it and he blew his top. Told me he won't be dictated to. He'll spend his money how and where he wants. We're supposed to be saving for our own place,' she said bleakly. 'At least, we were.'

'A few nights away might do him good. He'll appreciate you more.'

'You think?' She didn't look convinced.

'Where would you go?'

'Oh, there's an auntie of Bryn's. We go out to see her sometimes. Bit of a recluse, she is. She lives up in the hills all on her own. Been there all her life. It's really quiet. She's not used to company, but as long as you feed her and carry in the logs she's happy to have someone around.'

'Go,' I said. 'Let him stew in his own juice for a while.'

I couldn't settle to my sewing at the morning drop-in. Every few minutes I kept checking the window to see if there was any sign of Peter. Of course he'd take his delivery round to the back of the café so I doubted I'd see him. As soon as Kate suggested a coffee break, I took the chance to ring Rhiannon.

'He's not here yet. Any time now,' she said. 'I usually do coffee and a slice of cake for him. He always looks half starved.'

My stomach fluttered. Should I take the chance and leave now? There had only been a couple of people wander over to my table all morning to see what I was doing and ask about patchwork classes. Probably the weather, I thought. It hadn't stopped raining since I got here.

'I know it's early, but I think I'll pack up now,' I told Kate.

'It is a bit quiet, isn't it?' she agreed. 'You go on. If anyone's asking, I'll give them your schedule for the rest of the week.' She watched me start to pack away. Perhaps I looked relieved to be going.

'Everything all right?' she asked, studying me closely.

'Yes, fine. I just have a few things to do. You know what it's like, trying to get everything sorted. I need a few more quilts for the exhibition but it takes time getting round to see everyone.'

It wasn't exactly a lie, but I still felt uncomfortable as she smiled at me.

'You're doing a great job. Everyone's talking quilts,' she said.

I didn't see Peter's moped on the road as I headed out of Llannon. I slowed at the junction where the road split into three. To the right, the lane followed another smaller stream. Ahead lay the road over the hill towards Top Farm, Lloyd's place. Left lay the road over the bridge to The Garth. Where had the vehicle come from that had hit Willow? I could see Magda's face in the chemist's as I told her Willow had come out of the coma. She had been scared. Scared because of what Willow would remember?

I turned left and headed down to the bridge, then up through the woods and across the valley to The Garth. I slowed, anxiously searching for any sign of Peter's moped. Had he left for town?

'Mrs Beddows? It's Bronwen. I hope you don't mind, but I've come about your lovely quilts.'

I stood on the threshold, holding the loaf of *bara brith* I'd bought in the market. A little bribery never did any harm.

'Come on in. Peter's not here. He's doing his deliveries,' she said.

'That's OK. It was you I wanted to see. Shall I put the kettle on?'

With a pot of fresh brewed tea and a plate of buttered *bara brith* slices, I settled into the chair beside her.

'How's Willow? Is there any more news?' I asked her.

'Oh yes,' she said brightly. 'She's awake. Not that she can remember much of what happened, but at least now they say she's on the mend. I can't tell you how glad we are. It's such a relief for Peter. He's going up there later to see her.'

'It's all a bit of a mystery,' I said. 'Her leaving so suddenly like that.'

'She wasn't leaving. She was coming home,' she said.

'Home?' I stared at her. This wasn't the picture I'd had at all. No one had mentioned exactly which way she had been heading when the accident happened. I'd just assumed she was leaving. Running away, I'd thought. Even Peter had not corrected me. So exactly what was she doing on the road in the early hours of Thursday morning?

'Been out with friends, had she?' I said as casually as I could. But it was too late. The old lady had realised she had said too much. She munched slowly on the cake.

'Is there any more tea?' she asked mildly.

As I retreated to the kitchen to top up the pot, I looked out at the wide expanse of vegetable garden, the ploughed field beyond. Why had Peter not said where Willow had been? I pictured the junction again. The lane to the right, meandering between high hedges, following the line of the stream. Ahead, the road wound on over the hills, passing Lloyd's home. And left, the road that dipped down to the bridge then up the opposite slope of the valley towards the woods and The Garth. So, Lloyd's place. It had to be. She was coming back from Top Farm. So why hadn't Peter said so?

I carried the teapot back into the front room.

'I was in the Daisy Chain today. Lovely café. Very friendly. I gather Peter supplies them with eggs and veg.'

'Oh yes. Has done for years now. Lovely girl, Rhiannon. At one time, I'd hoped...' She sighed. 'They'd been at school together, you know. But it wasn't to be.'

'She must get busy in the summer. She said she had to take on extra help. Didn't Seren work for her some time?'

'That's right,' she said, nodding eagerly. 'It was working out well. Giving the girl more confidence. That's what she needed. Such a quiet little thing.'

'Did Willow ever work there?'

'No, no. She had enough to do.'

'Working on the garden, you mean?'

Again the old lady was silent. She took a sip of her tea.

'You said she brought the hens in most evenings. All except Wednesdays, wasn't it?'

'Did I?' she said, suddenly flustered. 'I don't remember. All the days are much the same to me.'

'Where did she work on Wednesdays then?'

'She didn't. Peter wouldn't allow it.'

'She wanted money though. Wasn't she saving up to go travelling, just like Seren?'

'That was different. That kind of work…' she said, contemptuous.

'What kind?'

She turned her head to me.

'I think you'd better go now. Peter will be back soon. He'll not be pleased to find you here.'

'I am trying to help him,' I insisted. 'What will help him most is the truth.'

'You think so?' she said, as if she didn't believe me.

I gave a sigh of frustration.

'At least may I take some pictures of your beautiful quilt? I saw it on your bed the other day when I was here. I'm cataloguing the heirloom quilts from the region. It would be great to include yours.'

'That old thing,' she dismissed.

'There's so much work gone into it. And the quilting patterns are worth recording. It'd make a great addition to the exhibition.'

'I suppose it'll do no harm,' she said reluctantly.

I took out my camera from my bag and went down the corridor to her room. The double quilt covering her bed was prettier than I remembered. The wholecloth quilt was intricately stitched with scrolls and leaves. Scissor shapes decorated the corners, a traditional Welsh pattern, and at the centre was a basket of stylised tulips. I flipped the cover over and took more photos. The light wasn't the best, but it was just good enough. All I then needed to do was take some details from her about when the quilt had been made, and about its composition. I guessed it was filled with an old woollen blanket for the wadding was smoother than if it had been stuffed with fleece.

When I had finished, I looked round for the half-quilt I remembered. That was the one that intrigued me most, for the quilting was not a traditional pattern at all. I remembered the curve of roses and leaves, the interwoven stems forming a heart. I'd seen nothing like it yet in all the heirloom quilts I'd seen around Llannon.

'How long ago would the bed quilt have been made? Can you remember?'

'We were always sewing,' she said. 'A little group of us. We helped each other make up quilts for our bottom drawer. That was before the war, of course. After that, with rationing, it was never easy to find enough fabric. That one must have been finished when I was about sixteen.'

'You shared the work with friends then?'

'Friends and family, yes, there were a few used to come to the farm. It was a chance to get together for a gossip as much as anything. There wasn't much else but hard work and Chapel.'

'And the other one? The half-quilt?'

'I don't remember,' she said flatly.

'You said your brother helped you with the quilt pattern.'

'Yes. He used to sit with us sometimes and watch us sewing. He'd see the quilting patterns we'd mark out on the plain cloth, and he said it couldn't be too hard. So one day he came in with a pattern he'd drawn himself.'

'The twining roses?'

'Yes,' she said softly. 'It was beautiful.'

'May I take a picture of it?'

She shook her head.

'Not that one,' she said. 'I couldn't have people looking at it the way it is.'

'But maybe if we found the other half?'

'No!' she said crossly.

116

I sighed. She was not going to budge where the half-quilt was concerned. I could appreciate she wanted to keep it safe when it meant so much to her: a memento of her dead brother. But it was an important piece of local textile history, too.

I took the empty plates and cups back into the kitchen and washed them. As I piled them onto the drainer, I heard the moped's engine putter into the yard. My glance flew in panic to the window. I had stayed too long. I hadn't meant Peter to find me here.

The kitchen door was flung open. Of course he recognised my car. He stood for a moment glaring at me, rage glowing in his eyes.

'I told you to keep away from here!'

'I brought Nan some cake. I wanted to ask about her quilts,' I said.

'You've asked. Now go.'

I nodded meekly. There didn't seem any point in arguing, and for now I could hardly ask him about Willow and what she'd been doing up at Lloyd's place the previous Wednesday evening.

'I'll just get my bag,' I said.

He marched ahead of me down the hall, only pausing to glance in at Nan. She was sitting with her head back, eyes closed, as if dozing.

'I told you she's not to come here,' he snapped.

'I thought there was no harm in it,' she said gently.

'I'll be the judge of that!'

He tugged open the front door as I gathered up my coat and bag. As I stepped outside, I saw another car turn in at the gate. The driver's door slammed, and a woman in high-heeled shoes came striding up the path to us. Her long cream coat flapped behind her, her bright lipsticked mouth was taut with anger. She marched past me, ignoring me completely.

'Peter Beddows, I take it?'

'What of it?' he challenged.

'You bastard!' She reached up and slapped him hard across the face. He jerked back. For a moment I thought he would hit out at her. Instead he merely stood his ground, glaring down at her.

'Who the hell are you?'

'Imogen's mother. Or, Willow, as you call her,' she said with contempt. Her face reddened with anger. 'What did you do to her?'

'I don't know what you mean,' he countered. 'It was an accident.'

'I'll bet! The police told me where to find her. My daughter. My poor baby!'

'It wasn't my doing!' he insisted.

'No? They might believe you. I don't! I've just been with her. She's saying nothing. Too terrified. But I'll get to the truth, don't you worry. I'll have you arrested. They'll make you confess!'

'I told you, I didn't hurt her. I'd never have hurt her.'

'You may fool the rest of them with your hippy peace-loving charade, but you don't fool me!'

Only now did she take notice of me standing in the porch.

'So who's this? Your latest?' she demanded. She turned to me. 'Get out, if you know what's good for you!' She was close to tears now, I could see.

'I told you. It wasn't me,' Peter repeated with icy calm. 'Look, why don't you come in. We can talk.'

'The only talking I'm doing is to the police. Thank God they found her letters. What were you going to do? Burn them all? Bury the evidence? Why did you stop her from posting them? She wanted me. I could have helped her.'

'But you didn't help her, did you? When she most needed you.'

'That's a lie!'

'Is it?' He glared at her. 'The letters,' he said patiently. 'Yes, she wrote them, intending to send them. But in the end she couldn't. She knew if she got in touch, you'd come and find her. She knew you'd only let her down again.'

'How dare you! I'm her mother!'

'And your boyfriend, what was his name? Graham? Still the love of your life, is he? You believed him rather than Willow, didn't you?'

'She was young. Immature. She was jealous of us, that was all. She thought she could split us up. When she ran away, I did everything to try and find her, to make it up to her.'

'Believing her would have been a start.'

'OK, so I was stupid. I thought Graham was the best thing in my life and Imogen was spoiling it. But I understand now, I know I was wrong. I want to make it up to her. And I will. I'll do anything to get her back.'

'So you're on your own now, are you? You thought you'd have another go at wrecking Willow's life. You sad cow.'

'Bastard!' she yelled again. 'You'd no right to keep her from me.'

'It was her choice,' he insisted. 'I tried to persuade her to contact you, but she'd made her mind up. And now I've met you, I know she was right.'

'You…' She raised her hand to strike him again, but this time he was ready for her and caught her wrist. He released his hold almost at once, as if scalded.

'Get off my land,' he said gruffly. 'I only wish I could stop you seeing Willow.'

'You can't!' she said in triumph. 'I'm her mother. And it's up to me who sees her. You stay away from her, you hear? I don't want you visiting her!'

She turned on her heel and marched back to her car, a mud-spattered BMW. She reversed none too steadily, grazing the gatepost as she swung the wheel, then, in a flurry of mud, she accelerated up the lane.

Peter leaned back against the door, his head bowing.

'You were right,' I said softly. 'She's a cow.'

'I've got to get to Willow,' he said then, stirring himself.

'You heard what she said. She'll do all she can to stop you.'

His glare was unyielding.

'I'm not the one who harmed her daughter,' he said. 'Willow needs my protection now more than ever.'

He swung away from me, heading off down the hallway.

'Peter!' I called after him. 'Tell me one thing. About Willow.'

'What?' he snapped.

'Was she up at Lloyd's the night of the accident?'

'Who told you that?'

'I sort of guessed,' I said.

'So what if she was?'

I remembered the way Magda had looked when I told her that Willow was out of the coma. That she might soon remember what happened that night.

'I think she may need protecting from more than just her mother,' I said.

'She was on her way home. It's got nothing to do with Lloyd,' he snapped.

'Can you be so sure?'

'I didn't like her going up there. I told her so. But she wanted the money. I wish I'd stopped her now,' he said bitterly.

'What happened?'

'That's just it. I don't know. Until she remembers, no one does.'

'Someone does,' I corrected him. 'Someone was driving the car that hit her. You've got to tell the police. Tell them where she was that night.'

'I can't!'

'Why ever not? It will at least clear your name.'

'No,' he said, almost pleading. 'Don't you see? I was out that night. The Land Rover... they know I drove it.'

'You were out?'

He nodded.

'I told you. I use it in emergencies. For Nan. There was someone she had to see. An old friend of hers. We were back later than we should have been. There was a road closed. The weather that night was dreadful. Buffeting wind, driving rain. I can't... I can't be sure it wasn't me that hit her.'

I stared at him, appalled, unable to speak. There was a fierce haunted look in his eyes. Was it true? Had he almost killed the girl?

'The windscreen wipers weren't working too well. I thought it was debris in the road. I didn't know. How could I have known? She always got a lift back. That night... I wish to God I'd never gone out,' he said, burying his face in his hands. 'It's a bloody nightmare.'

I heard the dull thud of a stick. Nan Beddows came out into the hall.

'Peter, you can't be sure,' she said. 'Willow's going to be all right. She'll remember what happened. She can tell us then what happened to her. It wasn't your fault.'

He turned his dark haunted gaze to me.

'But if it was me, if they send me to prison… what happens then?'

Without him to take care of her, his grandmother would have to go into a home. That was something neither of them wanted.

'Who was that woman?' Nan asked. 'I heard her shouting.'

'Willow's mother.'

Nan drew in a deep breath.

'She's got a nerve coming here.'

The two spoke quickly together in Welsh. I couldn't make out a word of it. Presently he nodded.

'OK, OK. But I'll ring the hospital anyway. They'll tell me how she is.'

I guessed he wasn't going to visit, not with Willow's mother on the rampage. Besides, he couldn't be sure what she'd told the police.

I retreated down the path. It was a week, I realised, since Willow had gone up to Lloyd's house. I turned back to Peter.

'Was it every Wednesday evening she worked there?'

He nodded.

'What did she do?'

'Waitressing, for his parties,' he said with evident contempt.

'And tonight?'

His eyes narrowed.

'Don't even think of it,' he said.

'All the same,' I shrugged, 'it would be interesting to have a look at some of the cars parked outside, wouldn't it?'

'Leave it!' he cautioned.

I nodded, accepting he was probably right. After my first and last visit to Top Farm, I knew I wasn't welcome. And with the CCTV cameras watching the drive, I'd probably not be allowed near the place. Lloyd's minders would see to that. Patience. Wait until Willow was better.

I was due back at Llannon's primary school that afternoon. The children had been busy making patchwork designs in coloured paper. I'd asked them to come up with some simple geometric designs, using the reds, greys and blacks that had once been the mainstay of traditional Welsh quilts using scraps of flannel. Most of the children had chosen to use a central diamond, framed by triangles, and bordered by narrower strips. Some had gone for a pattern of triangles within a border. We pinned the paper pieces onto cotton fabric in matching colours and then cut them out and stitched the pieces together to make their own mini patchwork, twelve inches square. Instead of making a quilt sandwich with wadding and a backing fabric, we stitched the finished blocks together, and had a large, boldly coloured quilt top that would cover a double bed. Next time I promised to teach them some quilting stitches.

As I drove back towards Newtown, heading home, I saw the sign for the hospital. I wondered if Peter had rung yet to ask after Willow. Poor guy. He was distraught at the idea that he might have knocked Willow down. And his anguish at the prospect of Nan having to go into a care home because of him was all too plain. Debris, he had said. Surely if he had hit Willow, he would have been aware of it? He would have seen her. Unless she was already lying in the road.

123

I pulled into the hospital car park. At reception I asked for the intensive care unit. Willow had been moved to a private room, the receptionist informed me. I followed the woman's directions and took the lift to the second floor. Down the corridor I saw a uniformed policeman sitting outside one of the side rooms. After Willow's mother's outburst, I wouldn't be surprised if they'd decided on extra protection. So much hinged on what Willow would remember when she woke up. I walked briskly towards him, clutching my bag and the couple of quilt books I'd taken from the back seat of my car.

'Library service,' I said, flashing the badge Kate had given me when I had first started in my post as Quilter in Residence. 'They told us Willow was conscious now.'

I had to gamble on the young constable not checking back with his superiors.

'Oh,' he said, scrambling to his feet. 'Don't know if she's up to reading, though,' he said doubtfully.

'Picture books,' I said with a confident smile. 'Helps the subconscious readjust.'

I pushed open the door.

I gave a sigh of relief. No sign of the harpy mother, though I had no doubt she wasn't far away.

Willow lay very still in the narrow bed, wired up to a monitor on the wall that blipped in time with her heartbeat and pulse rate. On top of the sheets her arm was encased in a plaster cast. With her dark red hair splayed out across the pillow, she looked very pale, except for the livid bruises down one side of her face, The skin was still puffy and raw where she had hit the tarmac. Her breathing was gentle, regular. Was she asleep?

'I've brought some books for you, Willow,' I said softly. 'Peter wanted to come himself, but your mother had other ideas.'

No response.

I lowered myself into the chair at her bedside. I looked at her hand resting on top of the bed cover. Should I reach out and touch her, let her know I was here? More than likely she didn't want me there. I was an intruder after all.

'How are you feeling?'

She gave a slight moan.

'Bloody awful,' she murmured, without opening her eyes.

So she was conscious. But did she know who I was?

'Can you remember what happened?'

She gave just the slightest shake of her head, frowning as she did so.

'It's a week ago now,' I said. 'Peter's worried about you.'

Did she smile then? It was so fleeting, I wasn't sure I hadn't imagined it.

'Always... worries,' she murmured.

I stood up. I shouldn't be there with her. Any minute now someone would walk in, demand to know what I was doing there, have me thrown out. Maybe arrested even. Depending how vindictive her mother felt.

'Willow, if there's anything you can remember, anything about that night, it might help Peter,' I whispered, bowing over her.

She turned her head slowly towards me. Her eyelids flickered open.

'They keep asking,' she said, her voice strained with exasperation. 'I told them. All I can remember is headlights. Blinding me.'

'That's OK,' I said, and touched her hand. 'You'll remember soon enough. We can wait.'

I turned, with relief, suddenly anxious to escape before I was discovered. That's when the door opened.

'Are you family?' the young nurse demanded, looking none too pleased to find me there with her patient.

'Library service,' I said, smiling, indicating the books I'd left on the table-top.

She frowned.

'It's late to be working, isn't it?'

'Volunteer,' I said. 'Have to fit it around my other job. Sorry. I'll be back to swap the books in a couple of days.'

I scurried out.

In the corridor I was aware of someone walking briskly towards me.

'You,' she said, as she passed me. She stopped and turned. I spun round to face her. Willow's mother. 'What the hell are you doing here? I warned Peter...'

'Just dropping off some books,' I said. 'Library service. Nothing to do with Peter.'

She glared at me, suspicious.

'I'm so glad your daughter's regained consciousness,' I said quickly. 'The sooner she remembers what happened, the sooner all this can be cleared up.'

'I can't believe it,' the woman said. I noticed she had replenished her makeup since she'd left The Garth. The eyeliner and eye shadow were perfectly applied. Not a hint of a smudge. And the cherry-red lipstick neatly followed the curves of her lips. 'Of all the places she could have ended up, and it's up there, in that... wilderness!' she snapped. 'After all she could have had with me.' There was a new light in her eyes. Something fierce and feral. She was staking her claim on the defenceless Willow, I realised. Any minute now she would insist on driving her home to take care of her.

'She hasn't remembered yet what happened?' I asked.

She gave a slight, bitter laugh.

'No, but her memory was always somewhat creative,' she said. 'I wouldn't set too much store by what she says.'

'All the same, someone almost killed her.'

She contemplated her answer for a moment. Perhaps she'd felt like doing that herself. Denial was all very well, but it took a lot of determination and self-delusion to hold out against your own child. I could only guess at how much of a personal attack she had felt at Willow's allegations. For her, a wealthy boyfriend was not to be given up easily, I suspected. It made a mockery of her judgement of suitable men. But dating women just to get at their children was nothing new. As she had belatedly discovered. She had a long struggle ahead to win Willow's forgiveness.

'That's why I insisted on police protection for my baby,' she said with a brave smile. 'And I certainly don't want Peter Beddows sneaking round here trying to influence her.'

'He didn't do it,' I said mildly.

'You think you know him?' she snapped.

'I know enough,' I insisted. 'And you would too, if you bothered to try and get to know him.'

'I've no intention…' she began haughtily.

I glanced at her briefly.

'That's the problem,' I said, and walked away.

Wednesday evenings. What exactly went on at Lloyd's parties? I wished I could have gone and seen for myself, but Peter was right. I'd never get near the place. Probably Lloyd would call a halt to the parties for the time being anyway. Far too inconvenient to risk a visit from the police.

Back at the cottage, I dug a frozen lasagne out of the deep freeze and waited for the microwave to ping. I opened a bottle of Chenin Blanc and filled my glass. I wondered what David Evans would rustle up for me tomorrow. I didn't like the sound of a 'light' anything. He was far too thin to be a good cook. All the same I was eager to hear if he'd found anything in the archives about a missing man.

I finished the lasagne, and carried another glass of wine into the studio. The quilt was hanging on the wall, the elf sisters smiling down at me as if they knew some vital secret I could only guess at. What did they know? The light danced in the beads and threads as I watched them. For a moment it was as if I saw them move, circling hand in hand as they danced. The more I thought about Willow and her mother, and Peter's dilemma, the more I felt I was at the centre of a swirl of doubt and uncertainty. Why had Peter's journey been such an emergency he had risked using the old Land Rover? What had he hit on the road?

In an effort to reinstate some order to the chaos of my imaginings, I made a start on binding the quilt ready for Friday's launch. I had in mind to do a simple bias binding for three edges, but the bottom edge was to be a free-fall of embroidered leaves and wispy cobwebs of fibre. I needed to sew the threads over dissolvable stabiliser. They needed to mesh closely together so that when the stabiliser was dissolved away, the threads still hung together like gossamer. It should look enchanting, rather than a hotchpotch of tangled threads. Just now, I doubted if I had the peace of mind to bring it off.

Perhaps tomorrow things would seem simpler. Perhaps David Evans would at least be able to solve the mystery of the bones in the landslip. But at heart I doubted there would be any solution at all.

12

THURSDAY

I had arranged with Kate to take two days out of my schedule to make sure the wall hanging was finished and delivered to the Forest Visitor Centre by midday Friday. I had no excuse to stop me working. I stitched, dissolved, threaded, cursed, but little by little the quilt was emerging, bound just as I had pictured it, with a tumble of veined leaves along the bottom edge. I stretched to ease my aching shoulders. Finished.

With little time to stop for lunch, I'd had a bowl of soup at midday and now, with David Evans' promise of a 'light supper' at six, by four o'clock I decided I needed to eat. While I mixed up an omelette, I switched on the radio. There was the usual traffic update, a weather forecast. No improvement in either case. The Penwern road was still closed. And there was a short item about the bones found in the landslip. As yet, they had not been identified. Police were asking the public's help.

'Some hope,' I thought. They'd have all sorts of cranks ringing in. I remembered what Willow's mother had said about her daughter's 'imaginative' memory. Though in Willow's case, what she remembered was more accurate, I suspected, than her mother would admit. What would happen to the girl now? And then there was Seren. Another mystery it would take some time to uncover if she didn't want to be found. I wondered how long Lloyd's parties had been going on. Was it possible Seren had gone there looking for work, just as Willow had done? Wanting to save for her travels. Why was she so desperate to keep her identity hidden? Peter must know.

I ran upstairs to dress for my meeting with David. It didn't feel right to call it a date. There was definitely nothing romantic in the air between us. I was far too modern for his tastes, I thought. But a quick glance in my wardrobe identified another problem. Tomorrow evening. The launch party at the Clun Forest Visitor Centre. Gabriel would be there. My stomach clenched. What was I going to wear? This was my one chance, maybe my last chance, to get Gabriel to make some kind of commitment, a promise for a future relationship once his family problems were resolved. I'd told him I would wait until he'd sorted things out. I knew it was going to be difficult for him, now that his daughter, Lydia, had every reason to avoid coming back here, but that wouldn't stop him returning. Not if he wanted to come back. It was up to me, wasn't it? I had to make sure he really wanted to.

I decided on black trousers and a comfortable jersey top in a forgiving cream and blue, and had just pulled on my jacket when my phone rang. As always, I found myself hoping it would be Gabriel, saying he was coming back sooner than expected, could we meet. But it was Peter. From the background noise, he sounded as if he were ringing from a pub somewhere.

'Willow's doing OK,' he told me. 'She says someone left her some quilting books.'

'Oh?' I didn't confess. 'Has she remembered anything about the accident yet?'

'She said all she can remember is headlights. Nothing else,' he said.

'Give her time. Something more will come back, I'm sure.'

'That's just it. Her mother wants her discharged. She says she can take care of her at home now, as it's just her broken arm that needs mending.'

'What? But she can't do that. Is that what Willow wants?'

'Right now I don't think she knows what she wants.'

'But you can't let her. Not after what happened.'

Peter sighed. 'Maybe she's right, though. It's time she and Willow got to know each other again. Worked something out.'

'Peter, I really don't think that's what Willow wants,' I said.

'Maybe not. But what can I do? They're not going to let her come home to me, are they? Not if they think I'm the one who nearly killed her.'

He hung up. I gave a sigh of frustration. What could I do? I could hardly march into the hospital and insist Willow be returned to The Garth. Besides, Peter had enough on his plate looking after the smallholding and his grandmother. And we were still no closer to finding out who the hit-and-run driver was.

I fumed for a while. Then I tried the phone again.

It was a weary DS Flint who answered.

'It's Bronwen Jones,' I said.

'Ah yes, the quilt lady,' he said. 'How can I help?' He actually sounded as if he meant it.

'I understand Willow's out of a coma now. Any time now she should remember a bit more about the accident.'

'So we're hoping.'

'In the meantime, I wondered if you'd made any more investigations.'

'Into what?'

'There are other properties on the road where the accident happened.'

'We have made enquiries,' he said guardedly.

'Including Top Farm, up on the hill?'

'Of course.'

'Lloyd was helpful, was he?'

He didn't answer.

'I just wondered, as it was a Wednesday night, and as Willow had been up at his place that evening, whether you had a list of all the cars that were there.'

'She was there?'

'Oh, perhaps Lloyd forgot to mention that, did he?' I asked breezily.

'If you have information for us, Miss Jones,' he countered. 'I'd appreciate a statement.'

'That's the problem. It's only what I've heard. I can't say I'm surprised no one else has mentioned it to you. Lloyd does seem to be a law unto himself round there.'

'Thank you, Miss Jones,' he said icily. 'Rest assured we'll do all we can to bring the perpetrator to justice.'

'Just ask him who was at the party, will you? They've got CCTV. It won't be hard to spot the cars,' I said, and hung up. It probably wasn't the wisest thing to have done, but just now it seemed the best thing from Peter's point of view, and Willow's. And the only way justice was ever going to get a look-in.

I set off, half an hour late, for my date in Llannon. I parked in a dark side street and found my way to the riverside terrace of tall stone-built houses that had once been homes for Llannon's weavers. David Evans looked somewhat strained. I knew I was late, but it wasn't entirely my fault.

'Do come in,' he said, with veiled impatience. 'Let me show you round the house before we eat. Though the food is almost ready. Here, let me take your jacket.'

'Thanks,' I said feeling like a schoolgirl chided by her teacher. Late again, Bronwen.

He was dressed much as I remembered from the museum, in a cream twill shirt under a rust-and-brown tweed waistcoat. His thin face looked somewhat flushed, presumably from cooking. I could smell something garlicky and rather good.

The ground floor was open-plan, with cream walls hung with the kind of blown-up photographs that adorned the walls of the museum. The back of the room was fitted out as a kitchen. A long oak table filled most of the space, with chairs piled with inviting tapestry cushions.

'Come on up. You'll want to see the quilts,' he said.

I followed him up the open wooden staircase to the small sitting room. It was too dark for any view of the river, but I could hear the rush and babble of water close by. With so much rain, the river had to be close to flood level.

'This is lovely,' I said, admiring the exposed beams, the tapestry pictures on the walls. There was a small sofa and a low coffee table heaped with books. On the wall behind, more books were ranged on pale oak shelves.

'Bedroom and bathroom over there,' he said nodding towards the far wall. 'My study's on the top floor. The old weavers' workshop. That's where I keep the quilts.' He gave a slight smile then, beginning to forgive me at last, relaxing a little. Perhaps our meal would not be so painful after all.

Another narrower staircase brought us to the second floor. I looked up at the low timbers that supported the roof, the pitched ceiling.

'The whole of the top floor would have been one big workshop, filled with looms,' he said. 'Hence the large windows, to make the most of the light. There used to be a staircase outside to lead straight up to the workshop, with the weavers' families all living on the lower floors. Now the houses are split up, mostly into flats. I was lucky to get this one all to myself,' he said with a shy smile.

As I crossed the polished wooden floor, I was aware of the slight sag of the timbers. I tried to imagine what it must have been like working up here all day: the skeins of dyed wool, the incessant clatter of the loom frames drowning out the music of the river, the shuttles skimming between the stretched warp threads, the dusty shreds of wool thick in the air. Maybe as many as twenty looms all crammed into that space under the eaves. Hard, relentless work, a skill perfected, and in its day no doubt a better wage than the farm labourers in the small hilltop farms could ever dream of.

There was a large mahogany desk under the window, hemmed in by files and books, and teetering piles of papers. I wandered towards it, tilting my head to try and read some of the book titles.

'My research,' he said, with a grimace, moving to stand before me, blocking out the clutter on his desktop. 'Slow progress, I'm afraid.'

'I'm sorry, I should have realised,' I said. 'I hope you didn't spend too much time checking the newspaper archives for me.'

Behind the rimless glasses, his eyes sparkled.

'It was a welcome distraction,' he said.

'Did you find anything?'

'Not yet,' he said. 'But I will persevere. And now, my quilts. What do you think?' He opened the door of a large cupboard in the corner, and carefully, reverently, took out the pile of quilts and unfolded them for me to admire. 'This is my favourite. I found it in a farm sale, about ten years ago. Been used as a horse blanket, I think. It has some wear, but still…'

I reached out and lightly touched the chequerboard border of black and scarlet. At the centre, a black diamond enclosed a scarlet heart.

'It's beautiful,' I said. I looked up and saw the warmth in his eyes.

'I'm glad you think so. It's the simplicity of the pattern that I like.'

'It looks very modern, that geometric design, and the strong colours,' I said.

'Timeless.' He turned away and just as carefully restored the quilts to the shelf in the cupboard. 'Shall we eat?' he said contentedly.

Over supper, I had to confess to him that I had not, as yet, had time to look at his folder of ideas, but David wasn't as upset as I'd imagined he would be. And he did cook well. The garlic mushroom soup was rich and creamy, and was followed by sea bass fillets with tangy ginger and lemon grass. For dessert there was a chocolate mousse that was at once rich and deep and feathery light.

'I hear the young lady from The Garth is making a good recovery,' he said, returning from the kitchen area with coffee.

'Thankfully, yes. They're hoping she'll soon be able to remember what happened. Strange, though. There was another girl who disappeared from The Garth about two years ago. Did you hear about that? Her name was Seren. I've seen her photo. She looked a little like Willow. Same dyed hair anyway, though she was younger.'

'Indeed?' he said. He sat suddenly upright, his long fingers locking together. 'Seren, you say?' He gave a little shake of his head. 'I don't recall.'

136

'She wasn't here for long, but I gather she worked in the Daisy Chain during the summer. I'm surprised you don't remember her.'

'Ah, pressure of work,' he said with a rueful shake of his head. 'I have little time to socialise. And my free time is taken up with my research.'

'I'd just love to find out where she went, and why. It would be such a help for Peter.'

He tilted his head to one side.

'How so?'

'Didn't you know? The police were up at The Garth just a couple of days ago. Searching for her body. They think Peter killed her and buried her somewhere.'

'Fools,' he said crisply. 'What evidence do they have?'

'I know. Everyone says Peter wouldn't hurt a fly.'

'Well, there you are then,' he said more easily. 'The girl took off, in search of pastures new. Who knows what gets into their heads?' He gave a smile, baring his prominent front teeth.

'I wish I knew,' I said.

'Another coffee? You've a long drive back,' he said. I took my cue. Evidently I was keeping him from his precious research.

'No thanks. I must go. I've a lot to do tomorrow. My big day.'

'Oh?'

'It's the launch for the Clun Forest Visitor Centre, and my quilt needs to be hanging in reception.'

He fetched my jacket and helped me into it. Just for a moment I felt his bony fingers rest on my shoulders. I suppressed a shudder.

'Safe journey,' he said softly, too close to me. I just prayed he didn't try and kiss me goodbye.

'Thanks. And I promise I'll get back to you about your ideas for the exhibition just as soon as I've had a chance to study your folder.'

I hurried out into River Walk, pausing only briefly to glance back. I saw him silhouetted in the doorway, a tall stooping figure, who raised his hand in farewell and then closed the door.

I couldn't be sure, but there had been a photo of a girl amongst the papers on his desk. I had caught a glimpse of a red-haired girl. His daughter? But Kate had said he wasn't married. Could it have been Willow, then? Why would he have a picture of her in his study?

13

FRIDAY

Last-minute panic. I woke early, well before it was light, uncertain about the beading, and whether the leaves were still intact on the bottom border. In my dreams it had become an ugly tangle, the whole quilt dissolving into cobweb threads. Downstairs in the studio, with the dawn still only a faint gleam over the hills, I flicked on the light and stared up at the wall hanging, holding my breath. Was it finished? Was it still in one piece?

I felt a surge of relief to find it still intact, hanging up on my wall. Then I felt sick. Too late to change anything now. It was an echo of the design I'd had in mind. My art was like that. It evolved as I worked on the quilt, using happy accidents, unexpected contrasts and clashes. At some point, the quilt took on its own identity, its own life, and I was simply there to bring it into being like a midwife. As the light caught the iridescent thread, the tiny beads, I could sense the movement in the fabric, of leaves tumbling, sunlight flickering through the branches, and the elfin sisters swaying in a ring as they danced hand in hand. I felt a tremble through me. Yes, I breathed, it was OK. I just hoped the rest of the committee would approve. That Gabriel would approve. More than anything, that Gabriel would approve, and not just of the quilt.

I ran back upstairs, my toast half eaten, and tugged open my wardrobe door. Whatever would I wear tonight for the launch? There was my usual standby of wide-legged black trousers and a silky printed top. Nothing too plunging or revealing. Nothing sleeveless. There were definitely elements of my body that needed a little camouflage. I just didn't do strapless or backless. Don't think I ever had. I pushed aside the silk top. There was a dark green full-length dress with a flattering cross-over top. I'd rarely worn it, and had been tempted a time or two to cut it up for a quilt. Only the distant memory of how much it had cost had prevented me. All the same, as I held it up against me, I seemed to bulge in all the wrong places. There had to be something else. Last summer, at the exhibition Gabriel had held at Cropstone Hall, I had felt, briefly, like a princess, in a long floaty printed dress, but a summer garden party was not the same as a chilly rain-soaked visitor centre at the edge of a forest. A plaid shirt and jeans would not look out of place, but I needed something that was both elegant and practical.

I showered and dressed quickly, in jeans and sweatshirt. If I hurried and checked over the quilt for any loose ends, stitched in its label with my details, gave the binding a final gentle press, I could get it to the Centre by midday. That would give me a couple of hours to shop in Ludlow and find something to wear for the launch. That, of everything, was the most daunting part. I hated trying on dresses. Hated the cramped cubicles, the harsh lighting, glaring mirrors. I always looked enormous, flustered and flushed. Perhaps I could send an apology. Say I was ill. Maybe Gabriel would come up to the cottage to see me instead. But could I risk it? What if he didn't come? He might just think I'd changed my mind about him and send me a text message. '*Sorry not to see you. Hope our paths may cross some other time.*' No, it was no use. I couldn't be that cowardly. I had to go. Go get him. Or risk losing him for ever. Lord, what a depressing prospect that was.

As I reached the new Visitor Centre, I felt a new anxiety. When I had last seen the building, it had had no glass in the windows, and no electrics, and the roof was yet to be planted up. If I'd been stressed about getting the quilt finished on time, I could just imagine how the builders must have been feeling. But the car park was newly gravelled, and two caterers' vans were parked by the main door. I hurried in, out of the relentless rain. There were carpenters still fixing screws into some of the cladding. In the main reception area, two men in Forest Centre T-shirts were setting up display boards while other volunteers were putting out wine glasses on the two long cloth-covered tables where the buffet would be set out.

'Hi, I've brought the wall hanging,' I said, as one of the flustered young women came past me carrying a box of glasses.

'Bronwen, is it?' she said, and smiled. 'That's a relief. Something's on time! Wait there. I'll go and find Gerald. I think he's in the kitchen sampling the food. I hope there's still some left.'

Moments later, the large bearded red-faced man I remembered from my interview with the Forest Trust committee came lumbering towards me.

'Bronwen! You made it. That's a relief. I'll get the boys to set up a ladder. You got the quilt there? Come on then. Let's see it unfolded.' He rubbed his hands gleefully, as if ready to dive into the buffet. Gerald Williams was in his fifties and knew the forest as well as if it were his own back garden. As a keen naturalist and photographer he'd been the dynamo in the long and wearying process of getting grants to build the Centre. It was his baby, and he looked every inch the proud father.

'Well. Who'd have believed it,' he said, standing back to admire the wall hanging as it was finally hoisted into place on the wall. His eyes glinted moistly. 'You've done us proud,' he said gruffly, giving me a bear-like hug. 'I loved the painting you did, but this, in the flesh, so to speak... well, it's more than I could have hoped for. It is sheer magic.'

I kissed him.

'Thanks, Gerald. I hope the rest of the committee will be as pleased.'

'Of course they will be!' he boomed. 'Now I must get on. Lots to do. Arses to kick. And don't forget we open at seven tonight with the speeches. We've got a few bigwigs coming along too, and the press. You'll be the star attraction.'

The thought terrified me. I hated being photographed.

'Then I'd better go and get scrubbed up,' I said. 'See you tonight.'

Ludlow, on a wet Friday afternoon, with the market in full swing in the square before the castle, was not the most relaxing of shopping trips. I tried a couple of boutiques but there was nothing that fitted, or if it did fit, it was a hideous colour. Considering I had a room full of gorgeous fabrics at home, it was ridiculous that I couldn't find anything I wanted to wear. I stopped for a coffee and chocolate cake in the café near the castle. It would help soothe my nerves, I told myself. I made my way down one of the streets towards the river, and found my favourite patchwork shop. A few minutes' drooling over the fat quarters wouldn't hurt, would it?

When I emerged with my bags some time later, it was getting dark. The market clock struck four. I felt a sudden panic. I was never going to get anything now.

142

What would Gabriel think if I turned up in last summer's print dress? He might take pity on me, and lend me his coat to stop me getting hypothermia.

I pushed my way through the market crowds, wondering if I had time to look in at the Rednal Gallery, just to see if they'd sold any more of my smaller art quilts. Though Clive, the owner, was still away in Barbados, his Russian assistant, the slender glamorous Irena, would be there. Pity I couldn't ask her for advice on what to wear. She always looked stunning.

I found myself in the yard leading to the gallery. There was a new shop opened, up a steep flight of steps. Some beautiful dyed silk scarves were draped in the window. I hauled myself up the steps, and peered in.

It was perfect.

I hadn't wanted to spend quite so much on the dress and neat bolero jacket, but it fitted beautifully, grazing lightly over my ample curves. Calf-length, the fabric was a shimmery silk jersey that rippled a dark wine-red. I felt fabulous.

'You shall go to the ball,' I breathed as I twirled in front of the cheval glass.

I reached the Visitor Centre just before seven. The car park was already half full. I could see groups of people in the main reception, holding glasses, chattering. I hated walking alone into social events.

'Bron, our star designer,' Gerald boomed, catching sight of me. He had made an effort to dress up. He had put on a corduroy jacket over his plaid shirt and jeans. Somehow he never looked entirely at home indoors, and now his face was redder than ever with the heat and the wine. 'You remember our committee people, of course. Let me introduce you.'

One of the volunteers, in a Forest Trust polo shirt under her black apron, arrived to take my coat. I emerged butterfly-like, feeling self-conscious. I tried to catch a glimpse of my reflection, for reassurance, in the now dark window panes that almost surrounded us.

Out of the crowd emerged a tall, slender young woman in a cream column of a gown, her skin smooth and perfectly tanned. Her blonde hair was cut short in a boyish style which admirably suited her finely boned face. I felt deflated. How could I possibly think I looked attractive? I sighed, and reached for the hand she was holding out.

'I'm so pleased to meet you,' she cooed, a distinct American drawl in her voice. 'Gabriel's been telling me what an amazing artist you are. Now I've seen the proof for myself,' she said with a nod towards the quilt behind us on the wall.

'Gabriel?' I queried, my mouth suddenly dry. 'He's here?'

'Of course. He wouldn't have missed this,' she said, with an enveloping smile. And somehow he was there, and I hadn't seen him. His arm slid around me, and I was looking up into those dark and sparkling eyes.

'Gabriel…' I got out, stifled.

'Good to see you,' he murmured, his lips far too close to my ear. His warm breath sent a tingle running through me. He drew away. 'This is Carly, my new PA.'

'Good to meet you, Carly,' I said, digging out a smile with an effort. No amount of designer dresses were ever going to compare with her tanned, superbly honed body. I wished now I hadn't come. I had a sick icy lump in my stomach.

144

'Let me get you some wine,' Gabriel said, turning away.

'I must say, I just love your quilt,' Carly gushed. 'You really have an amazing talent. My Mom is a quilter too, but nothing in your league. She'd love to meet you.'

'Thanks,' I said, miserably. So now I was old enough to be her mother, was I?

'Here.' Gabriel handed me a glass of chilled white wine. I hardly tasted it, draining it in a few gulps. It didn't do much to steady my nerves. I looked round for some way of escaping. But I could see Gerald steering some suited dignitary my way. The local mayor, I guessed, from the gold chain of office. And in the midst of all the introductions and handshakes, a camera flash went off. I'd forgotten about the press. Had I been holding my stomach in? I bet my cheeks were flushed.

I looked round after our brief chat only to find Gabriel had disappeared again. Mingling, no doubt. He was good at that. I sighed, and headed for the table to refill my glass. I wondered how long it would be till we ate. I'd not had anything since the chocolate cake, and I was already feeling distinctly light-headed.

As I turned back, sipping wine, I saw with relief a couple of the Centre volunteers emerge from the kitchen with trays of nibbles. I sidled round a couple of groups of people, heading for the food. I was starving.

'I hear you're Quilter in Residence over in Llannon,' someone said close by. I had to stop and chat for a moment. I remembered the woman from the committee. I told her about the exhibition we were planning for the end of my tenure.

'I've managed to find some really beautiful heirloom quilts, but I'm always on the lookout for more,' I said.

'You should go on the radio. I'll set it up for you. Evan,' she called, turning from me. She summoned a tall, thin young man in a jacket that hung loosely from his shoulders. 'You'll do an interview with Bronwen, won't you? She's looking for old quilts,' she said. Evan took my details. He presented a lunchtime programme on the local radio, he said.

'Just our sort of thing,' he beamed rather toothily. 'Local interest. Come along to the studio next week. I'm doing a piece on the Visitor Centre launch on Monday, so if you can come in Tuesday, that would tie in well.'

'Thanks. It would be a help,' I said. I would have time on Sunday to prepare some notes. 'Have you heard anything about the bones that turned up in the landslip at Penwern? I wondered if anyone had got in touch. He must have been a local man, don't you think?'

'Quite a mystery,' he agreed. 'We've had a few people phoning in about long-lost relatives. I've passed all the info on to the police, of course, but I don't think they're any closer to finding out who it was.'

'Somebody knows,' I said, sipping the last of my wine.

He nodded sagely, his eyes bright.

'Intriguing, isn't it? Here, let me get you a refill.' He took the glass from me and made off through the crowd before I could stop him. I'd have to ditch it in favour of a soft drink if I was ever going to drive home.

I looked round but still couldn't see Gabriel. There was a second room, leading off from the reception, where I could see display boards depicting the area's history and wildlife. He was probably in there. As I made to go to look for him, I caught sight of a familiar face watching me from the doorway with a none too friendly expression: Lloyd. What was he doing there? I

146

noted Magda wasn't with him, but I'd just bet he had one or more of his minders chained up in the car park.

'Here we are,' Evan said cheerfully. 'Bottoms up.'

Hastily I took the glass from him and pushed my way forward to the exhibition room.

'I don't think I've seen these,' I said, aware that Evan was following me, a now rather startled expression on his face.

'Oh, right,' he said, casting about him at the woodland mural on the walls, the display panels showing the forest's history. There were a few people in here. Gabriel wasn't among them, I noted. 'You OK?'

'Just a bit hot out there,' I said, blushing.

'Ah,' he said wisely. I'm sure he'd done phone-ins about the menopause. It was easier than having to explain about Lloyd.

'I'm not sure I know many people here,' I said. 'One or two I know from the committee. The chap that just came in, in the shiny suit. I think I've seen him around Llannon.'

Evan craned his head back to peer over the crowd.

'Ah, you mean Lloyd,' he said and gave a knowing smile. 'Yes, I'll bet you've seen him around. Owns the town, doesn't he? His little fiefdom.'

'So what's he doing here?'

'Looking for some respectability,' he said drily. 'He likes to be thought a patron of the arts and good causes. Makes up for all the grubby little enterprises he's mixed up in. But don't quote me on that.'

'No,' I said, alarmed. 'Just exactly what sort of enterprises?'

'Lap-dancing clubs, strip joints, and gambling, mainly. All good clean fun, I'm sure.' He sounded

147

jaunty but he wasn't smiling. 'Not a man to cross, they say.'

'Oh. Well, I'll bear that in mind.' I glanced out at the crowd again. I could see Lloyd talking to someone, his back turned to me, but he was looking round all the time as if searching for me. There was no way I was going to chance fetching a soft drink while he was there waiting to pounce. 'Actually I was hoping to have a word with Gabriel Haywood. He's one of the main benefactors for the Centre, isn't he?'

'Well, his bank is,' Evan said. I sensed he didn't give Gabriel too high an approval rating either. 'I wonder what they get out of it, turning up at provincial beanfeasts like this. Ego, probably.' He gave a sigh. 'All an elaborate tax dodge, I shouldn't wonder. Investing in forests. Reduces their tax liability.'

I smiled. 'You're such a romantic.'

'You've got me sussed,' he said, smiling back.

'I'd better mingle. Thanks for the drink. I'll see you next Tuesday,' I said, edging away. 'What time?'

'One o'clock. On the dot.' He raised his glass in salute.

I made my way down the room and found myself in a corridor. Ahead were the toilets. I darted into the ladies' loo. At least I could splash some cold water on my face and cool my complexion. I stared at myself in the mirror. Who was I kidding? Why ever did I think Gabriel would look twice at me? By now my feet and back were aching. I hated having to wear high heels. I slid my feet out of them, just for a glorious minute or two of freedom, and bent down to rub the circulation back into my toes.

The door banged open. I looked up in surprise at the noise.

Lloyd was standing there, his back against the door, blocking my escape.

'It seems you didn't understand me, Miss Jones,' he said in that quiet, high-pitched voice. 'I told you to keep out of my affairs. And now you send the police sniffing around. It was you, wasn't it? No one else would have been so stupid.'

I straightened, still holding my shoes. How good a weapon would they make? Pity they weren't stilettos.

'If you've done nothing wrong, you've nothing to be afraid of,' I retorted.

'Afraid?' He gave a soft chuckle. 'You think I'm afraid?'

'Aren't you? What did happen to Willow after she'd been working at your place? You know, don't you? You've got her on CCTV.'

He tipped his head to one side.

'Sadly, we hadn't kept the tapes from that week. No need to store them if there's nothing of interest, is there?'

'But she was there.'

'And she left about midnight. She didn't want a lift. She insisted on walking home.'

'Who else was there? Who left soon after she did?'

'No one, Miss Jones,' he said darkly. 'You got that?' He took a step nearer, grabbed hold of my arm, his hand curled around my throat. 'Why don't you ask that boyfriend of yours what he was doing out on the road that night?'

'Peter didn't hit her.'

'Sure, are you?'

I tried to shrug away from him. Although he was no taller than me, he was a great deal stronger. I could feel his fingers tighten their grip. I stared at him, my heart pounding.

'It wasn't Peter,' I insisted.

'Very protective,' he said, his lips close to my face. His blue eyes shone with a keen flame. 'Keen on him, are you? Makes you hot, does he? Randy little sod like him? Willow's the second girl he's had up there you know. What happened to the first one, then?'

'Seren? She left. Went travelling.'

'That what he told you?' He chuckled softly. 'Believe that, you'd believe anything. Be careful, Miss Jones. Don't want the police having to search for a third one, do we?'

His hand glided away and pinched my bottom.

'Pity you've teamed up with the wrong side. I don't mind them a little on the fleshy side sometimes. A bit of variety, you know?' he leered. 'Spice of life. And I like a lot of spice in mine. Enjoy your evening.' Still grinning, he nodded, and let himself out, closing the door on me.

I leaned back on the handbasin, feeling weak and scared. My body was shaking. He had such an air of menace that even if he hadn't hurt me, even though the threats were vague, insubstantial, there was a real promise in them that terrified me. But I was more than ever convinced he knew exactly what had happened to Willow. The problem was, finding out the truth.

I sprinkled some water on my face, checked my reflection. There were still the reddened impressions of his fingers at my throat. I tipped the rest of my wine down the sink. Slowly I coaxed my feet back into my shoes and tottered out to join the party. The noise of laughter and people chattering was louder than before. I heard Gerald's voice boom above the rest.

'Ladies and gentlemen, your attention please.'

I halted. He was just about to start on the speeches and the official opening. He'd be looking round the room for me now, but the last thing I wanted was to be the centre of attention. I wanted just to creep away unnoticed, to go back to my cottage.

'Bron, where have you been hiding? I've been looking everywhere for you. I was beginning to think you'd gone home!'

Gabriel was beside me, his arm slipping round my shoulders.

'I... was in the loo. I hate these formal dos, don't you?' I said with forced brightness.

'I guess I'm used to them by now. Can I get you a drink?'

'Lord, no!' I said hastily. 'I've had my quota. I've got to drive home,' I said. 'But if there's any food...'

He smiled, raised his hand and moments later, out of the crowd, came one of the young waitresses with a tray of puff pastry squares topped with mushroom duxelles, and chicken goujons.

'Here,' he said, settling down on the foot of the wooden staircase that led up to the offices. He tapped the space beside him. I sat. 'You know I have to go back to the States shortly.'

I nodded. 'How is Lydia?'

'On an even keel for now, but you know I have to be there with her. At least for now.'

'Of course. Any news on the house sale?'

'It'll be a while. I'm in no rush.'

'No, I suppose not.'

'But I'll miss it, you know. The horses, the hills, the countryside. And you, more than anything.'

'Me?' I breathed, my heartbeat hammering.

'I'm so grateful for all you did, helping sort things out with Lydia.'

'Oh. That.' I shrugged.

He hugged me against him.

'If we'd just had more time,' he sighed.

'Gabriel?'

I looked round and saw Carly. She was holding a mobile phone.

'Do you mind? I have to take this. It's Liddy,' he said. He got to his feet and took the phone from Carly. As he wandered back into the exhibition room to talk to his daughter, Carly was left watching me.

'He's a really terrific dad, you know,' she said.

'I know.' I smiled.

'A great guy.' She watched him keenly. I followed her gaze. He glanced up from his call, but it was her eye he caught. He gave a smile, an almost imperceptible wave, like a secret signal between them. And I knew then that she was more than just his new PA.

'Excuse me, I have to…' I abandoned my plate on the bottom of the stairs and almost ran back down the corridor, past the toilets, to the fire door, and let myself out into the cold and driving rain.

I sat in the Land Rover for several minutes, the rain streaming down the windscreen, blinded, as the tears coursed down my face. What a fool I'd been. A fool to think a man like Gabriel would ever look at me. Not when he could have the likes of Carly, half my age and probably half my weight. Fool! I thudded my fist against the steering wheel.

I started the engine, flicked on the lights.

In the sudden glare, I could see two shadowy figures standing against the silver Mercedes. Lloyd, and one of the waitresses. He had her pinned against the door, her skirt lifted high enough to expose her white thighs. Moments later, the car door swung open and she tumbled inside onto the back seat. He looked round, grinning, aware that I was watching him. I glared in fury. But there was nothing I could do.

I revved the engine and spun the car into reverse. As I drove away, I glimpsed the figure running out of the Centre.

'Bron!' Gabriel called.

I didn't, couldn't, stop.

14

SATURDAY

When I woke the next morning, my new dress and bolero jacket were scrunched in a heap on the bedroom floor. My head thumped as if I had a hangover. I reached out reluctantly and checked the clock; it was nine. I had a workshop at the library at two. I fell back on the pillows and didn't want to move. I didn't want to face anyone.

I had lost all hope of a relationship with Gabriel. How could I have been so stupid? What was wrong with me? Maybe the truth was I really didn't want anyone in my life. I had only wanted Gabriel because I knew I couldn't have him. I wouldn't have to face any conflict in my life. I had my fabrics, my design work, and my lovely cottage. I should be content, like Vi, and enjoy what life offered. Perhaps I should get a dog.

'So how did it go?' Vi asked when I ambled down to Apple Tree Cottage after breakfast. My ego still felt bruised, and I wasn't sure if Lloyd's fingermarks were still visible at my throat. Psychologically I could still feel his hold on me.

'Don't ask,' I groaned, and promptly started to tell her.

Vi made another pot of tea and offered me the plate of chocolate brownies.

'So you're sure he and Carly are together?'

'There was no mistake,' I insisted. 'I could read the signs.'

'Can't blame him. You didn't exactly give him much encouragement,' she said.

'Short of rolling onto my back and kicking my legs in the air, I'm not sure what else I could have done,' I snapped.

'How was your date with the museum guy?' she asked.

'It wasn't a date!' I protested. 'He's very tied up in his work. Perhaps a bit too much. He seems very lonely, rather sad, I thought. But he does have some good ideas for the exhibition. Town trails, for example. Walking tours. Oh, and the quilts he's got are just gorgeous.'

'Are you seeing him again?'

'It's strictly business,' I said. 'Besides,' I shrugged, 'there was something odd. I don't know, it may be my imagination. But I thought there was a photograph of Willow on his desk.'

Vi looked sternly at me.

'You're sure?'

'Well, it was only a glance. I can't be sure. But it did look a bit like her.'

'Now why would he have her photo, do you think?' she said. 'Got a car, has he?' she said then, her eyes brightening.

'Oh Vi, you can't think that... I mean, he's a bit sad, but I hardly think he'd have tried to run her down.'

'Unrequited love?' she said sharply. 'He sounds just the obsessive type that would do something like that if she'd rejected him.'

I shook my head.

'He's too mild-mannered for that,' I said.

She gave a short sigh.

'Perhaps it'd be best you don't meet him alone again,' she said. 'So how is the girl anyway? Making progress?'

'When I saw her, she said she still can't remember much. Only the glare of headlights. It'll take time.'

'And in the meantime everyone's blaming Peter?'

'Trouble is, he believes it. He said he was out, in the Land Rover. He felt the car hit something on the way back. I'm sure it couldn't have been Willow. The time was wrong. Peter was back before midnight. I just can't prove anything.'

'Has he said anything more about Seren?'

'It's as much a mystery to him as to anyone. He said she had good reason to cover her tracks. She didn't want to be found. I don't even know if that's her real name. Did I tell you, Willow's mother calls her Imogen?'

'Someone must know where Seren went to,' Vi insisted.

'I tried asking Lloyd, but he claimed not to have known her. What more can I do?'

'Patience. The police are doing all they can,' she said, intending to reassure. Having met DS Flint, I wasn't at all sure they were looking any further than The Garth.

'There has to be some way of finding her,' I said, but without much hope.

As I shut the garden gate behind me and started up the lane, I saw there was a car parked outside my cottage. A sporty Jaguar. Gabriel's car. My heartbeat started racing and I quickened my pace. As I drew level, the driver's door opened. Gabriel stepped out, straightening slowly, his arm resting on the open door.

'You left your coat behind, Cinderella,' he said, unsmiling.

'Oh. Yes. Thanks,' I muttered, aware that I was beginning to blush.

'You took off in a hell of a hurry. You didn't even come and say goodbye. Something wrong?'

I stared up at him, into those shining dark eyes. So what was I going to tell him? The truth? That I'd seen him and Carly together and realised I was no match for her youth and beauty?

'Sorry. I... didn't feel too good. Too much wine on an empty stomach,' I said.

He bent into the car and reached for the coat from the passenger seat.

'May I?' He draped it round my shoulders, and pulled me closer against him. 'If I didn't know you better, I'd say you'd run away.'

My blush deepened.

'Would you like a coffee?' I said, glad to turn away from him and avoid that all too searching gaze.

He locked the car and followed me into the cottage.

Now what was I going to do? Play hostess, avoid all mention of Carly?

'Are you going to tell me the truth now?' he said when he had sat down at the table in the kitchen and I had finished fiddling with the kettle, coffee jar and mugs.

I glanced at him. There seemed no escape. Nowhere I could run to this time.

'Last time you were here,' I said softly, 'you said something about 'us'. About wanting to be part of my life. I think, last night, I realised it was never going to happen.'

I stood at the opposite side of the table, facing him. I felt it was the bravest thing I'd ever said.

He bowed his head.

'You had so little faith in me?'

'I'm just being realistic,' I said. 'When I saw you and Carly...'

'Ah. That's it. I rather thought it might be,' he said. He pushed up from the table and came round the corner to me. His hands reached out and held me lightly by the shoulders. 'She's an adorable girl, but she's thirty years younger than me. Easy on the eye, I admit, but what would she ever see in an old fossil like me?'

I gazed wearily back at him. Did he really expect me to believe that? I knew plenty of young women with older, richer boyfriends. He was beginning to sound like Ed, ready with a plausible reason for his every action. Excuses unlimited. I felt chilled with disappointment. I had thought Gabriel was different. Besides, whatever did he see in me?

'It's OK. I'm a big girl. Literally. I'm not upset because you're leaving.'

His hands dropped to his sides.

'Then I've misunderstood. Completely. I'm sorry,' he said. 'I'd better be going.'

'Gabriel… it wasn't a misunderstanding,' I blurted out. 'But what was I supposed to think?'

He gave a deep sigh.

'I couldn't turn my phone off because Lydia was due to ring and I was expected to give a speech at the launch. I'd promised Liddy I'd always be there for her, that my phone would always be on. If that meant Carly taking the call and holding on for me, so be it. I wouldn't have brought her along otherwise. She's engaged to a young Adonis in New York. When we get back to the States, I'm invited to their wedding. OK?'

'OK,' I said, blushing all the more.

He shook his head.

'Why do you belittle yourself like that? Don't you know just how great you are?'

I resisted the 'size' retort and hung my head.

'After what I went through with Ed, I suppose I'm just wary,' I said. 'It's difficult to believe in love again.'

'Try,' he said.

This time, as he put his arms around me, I did not duck away.

There had been no time to get lunch, though I felt far from hungry. Discovering exactly how much Gabriel loved me and my body made me feel thoroughly at peace with the world. He was coming back to me. He had promised that. There would be a time, soon, when he would be part of my life. I just had to be patient and wait for him.

The afternoon workshop in the library was quiet. A few of the children from the weekday session came along with mums and grandmothers in tow. We painted and stamped some fabrics, stitched the pieces together, and this time used some of the wool the children had collected to make the wadding for the quilt.

I finished at four. When I checked my phone there was a text from Gabriel. A smiley face and lots of xxx's. I smiled back, my stomach doing a little somersault. It was going to be tough waiting for him to come back.

I packed up the car and walked down to the market to see Rachel. There were few shoppers at that hour, and she was starting to pack away her stall.

'How are you?' I asked her. She looked anxious, I thought. I wondered how well the truce was holding between her and Bryn. The yellow bruising still dominated her small pale face. I noticed her black hair was slicked down with gel into a no-nonsense style.

She shrugged. 'I wish I'd moved out when I could. I just don't think I can stand much more of him storming round like a bear with a sore head.'

'I thought you'd sorted things out.'

'It isn't that simple,' she said.

'Here, let me take one of those,' I said, reaching for the box she had packed up. 'Your car out the back, is it?'

She nodded. I followed her down through the market and out through the side door to the small crammed car park behind the market building where her Mini was parked.

'I don't know what to do,' she said bleakly.

'About Bryn? Moving out sounds like a good plan,' I suggested. She gave a shake of her head.

'I can't leave him now, Bron. He's in trouble. Real trouble. That's why he's being such a pain. And right now I don't see any way out of it.'

'What's he done?'

'Oh, it's his own stupid fault. Got in with the wrong crowd, you know? Boys' night out. It was great at first. A big party. Drinking, gambling. They played poker. He had a few good wins. Beginner's luck, I reckon. But since then... He owes thousands. And there's just no way he can pay him back.'

I stared at her, appalled.

'You mean, Lloyd? He owes Lloyd?'

She nodded. I let out a low curse.

'I can't bear it. He's tried talking to him, promising to pay him back bit by bit, but Lloyd's being an arse about it.' She slammed the boot of her car and stood with her arms wrapped round herself. 'Lloyd wants his money. He knows Bryn can't pay him. I'm scared he'll make Bryn do something stupid.'

'Like what?'

160

'That's just it. Bryn won't talk about it. But I know he's been up there to see Lloyd. I know they're planning something. I can't stop him, Bron. He won't listen to me. There's nothing I can do.'

I hugged her.

'Hang on in there. Try and find out what's going on. Maybe Magda knows something. Just let me know if I can help, OK?'

She nodded meekly, tears standing in her eyes. She was scared, and from what I knew of Lloyd, I could understand why.

The daylight was fading rapidly as I drove out of Llannon. I turned over the bridge and pulled up near the police sign. Even if there was nothing I could do to help Bryn, I had a chance at least of helping Peter. I got out of the car and walked down the road, checking the verges for a dead badger, maybe, or a fox. Anything that Peter's Land Rover might have hit. I knew it was a remote chance of finding anything. It was over a week since the accident, but still I had to be sure. I leaned over the farm gate in case anything had been tossed into the field, but there was nothing.

I reached the bridge, peered down into the rush of water. The river was high, close to the top of the banks. Plenty of debris there, swept along by the swirling current: branches, tree stumps, plastic bags. But nothing that could help Peter's cause.

I headed back up the hill. In amongst the meshing hawthorn branches of the hedge were pale straws. A lot of them, I realised. There were more caught up in the grass and mud of the verge. I studied them for a moment, then got back into the car. I started the engine and this time took the tight right-hand turn at the junction.

161

I followed the narrow lane that curved and twisted its way across the hillside. Around a bend I saw a field with a couple of horses out grazing. I pulled up in the gateway. There was mud everywhere, trampled by hooves and deeply scored with tyre treads. In the corner of the field was a stable with a galvanised roof. Through the open door, I saw the floor was covered with straw. And just by the door, under black polythene, was a stack of straw bales. I let out a soft 'yes'. At the junction the road was muddy with soil washed down from the fields as well as brought on tractor wheels. And the turning was tight. Someone had brought those straw bales up for the horses, maybe on a tractor or truck. What if a bale had fallen off at the turning? If that was what Peter had hit, he would certainly have felt the impact.

I glanced round. There was no sign of any house nearby. Then I noticed a thin plume of smoke snatched and whirling on the wind. It was just beyond the stand of trees at the next bend.

I pulled up in the driveway of a long brick bungalow. A rickety conservatory stood to one side, where shrivelled plants still remained as evidence of warmer days. Glancing back, I saw there was a great view along the valley down to the town. The young woman who came to the door was in no mood to deal with strangers turning up unannounced on her doorstep. She was barefoot, and wearing black leggings, her hair covered in a towel. From the slight drip coursing down her face, I could see she was in the middle of dyeing her hair a deep chestnut.

'Sorry to disturb you, only I just stopped at the field down the lane. I was wondering about the horses,' I began.

'What about them?' she snapped.

'There are some straw bales by the stable.'

She nodded. 'A friend of mine gets them for me,' she said, glaring at me. 'You want him to get you some?'

'No, no, I haven't any horses,' I said hastily. 'But could you tell me when exactly he brought them?'

'Why?'

'Please, if you could just remember?'

She gave an impatient sigh.

'The last lot? A week ago Wednesday I think. Yes, it was one evening after work. He'd promised me six bales but there were only five.'

'Where was the sixth one?'

'Someone nicked it, he reckoned. He swore it was on the truck when he left. Only when he got here, it had gone. Probably fallen off the back of the truck on the way.'

At the junction, I thought, when he took the turning too fast, perhaps slithering in the mud on the road. And sometime later, after midnight, Peter had hit it with his Land Rover.

'He comes up from the Llannon road?' I asked. 'Only, it looks like there's some scraps of straw in the hedgerow.'

'No, he comes over the hill from Brynmawr. Why?' she said, frowning.

Driving downhill, he'd taken the sharp left-hand bend a little fast perhaps, on a muddy road. And the bale had toppled out. So why hadn't he seen the bale on the way back, I wondered?

'Your friend, about what time did he get here?'

'Must've been about eight. Why?'

'And he drove back the same way?'

'I suppose. Not straight away, mind. He... he stayed a while,' she said, starting to blush. A colour that

163

clashed somewhat with the chestnut dribble down her cheek. I nodded. I didn't bother asking if her parents had been out that night. I bet he picked up the bale when he went home, just after midnight, and hadn't thought to tell the girl. It hadn't seemed important. Only it could be crucially important to Peter.

'Thanks,' I said. 'You've been a great help.'

'I have?' She gave me a puzzled look and slowly closed the door.

'I think I've got good news,' I said as Peter came across the yard towards me. I could see from his expression he didn't want me there. He wiped his hands on a rag tucked in his belt.

'That'll make a change,' he said glumly.

I followed him into the kitchen, pulled off my muddy shoes and went to say hello to Nan.

'So what's the news then?' he asked when he joined us.

'I found some straw bales,' I said. 'At least, there was one missing. Someone was dropping them off at a field just beyond the junction where Willow's accident happened. I think one of the bales fell off in the road. That's what you hit with the Land Rover.'

'You're sure?'

'Pretty much. I asked about it at the house.'

'Hughes' place.' He nodded and turned to his grandmother. 'Their girl's got a couple of ponies up there.'

'I hope we don't have to prove anything to the police, but just in case... I really wanted to find out for your peace of mind more than anything else,' I said.

He swallowed.

'Thanks,' he said huskily. 'It means a lot to me.'

'How is Willow? Is there any more news?'

'I rang the hospital when I was in the town this morning. She's doing OK, they say. I don't think she's remembered much else yet. I just wish that bitch of a mother would back off. She's got no right to keep me away from her. It was her Willow was getting away from to start with!'

I didn't choose to remind him that the police were also none too keen on letting him near Willow. Not while he was still a suspect in the accident.

'When I was in the café last week, I talked to Rhiannon,' I said. 'She knew Seren, didn't she? The girl had worked for her.'

Peter nodded.

'From what she said, I gather Seren had been unhappy at home, too. Can you tell me anything about her? It might help us find where she's gone to.'

'You won't find her. Not if she doesn't want to be found,' Peter said doggedly. He got to his feet. 'Sorry, I've got work to do. Can't sit around chatting.'

'Peter, make the young lady some tea, at least,' Nan chided. 'She's come all this way.'

Peter glared at me, in no mood for hospitality.

'Let me give you a hand,' I said brightly.

I followed him into the kitchen. I could sense he didn't want me there. I might have helped him, but he hated me for it. He didn't want to be in debt to me. Sometimes, I could see, his stubborn independence would be exasperating. Especially to a young girl like Seren, or Willow.

'Peter,' I began.

He clattered the mugs onto the worktop, then span round to face me, his face tense with an anger that flared in his eyes.

'You can't help us, all right? We'll manage!'

'And Seren? Will she manage?'

165

'I hope so,' he muttered. 'Though now, thanks to you, I'm not so sure. You could have ruined everything. Why did you have to tell the police about her?' he demanded. 'What business was it of yours?'

'She was missing!'

'Because she wants it that way!'

'Are you so sure?'

'Yes!' he shouted. Then more softly, 'Yes. You don't know. You don't know what harm you may have done.'

'Then tell me,' I insisted.

I sat down, my arms folded on the table-top, and waited. He stood with his back to me, leaning on the sink, staring out through the window at the yard. I heard him sigh.

'She had a tough time, growing up. Her mum was on drugs. Seren had a string of foster parents. When she was fourteen, she got in with a bad crowd. Her foster parents couldn't cope. They chucked her out. She spent the last two years in a home. She was shoplifting, drinking, didn't care what she did. Then as soon as she was sixteen, she was out of there. Freedom, she thought. Only her so-called friends had other plans for her. Drugs, selling her body. She stuck it for a while, then her best friend died. Overdose. Seren knew it would be her next if she didn't get away. But she knew too much. If she was out of their control, she could hurt them, put them in prison. That's when she ran. Before they could stop her. She took up with some musician. He was busking, travelling round. And one day she found herself here, at the folk festival. It was like Paradise, she said. She was clean then. Hadn't done drugs for a while. She just wanted a chance, you know? To be herself. She deserved that, didn't she?'

'So why did she take off again?'

He shrugged.

'I always knew she would. I just didn't think it would be so soon.' He turned and faced me. 'Now her picture's out there. If the police find her, so will they.'

I shivered.

'I'm sorry. I'd no idea.'

He glanced back out of the window at the darkening sky.

'Thailand, she always wanted to go to Thailand. I just hope she got there. Out of their reach.'

I said nothing, gripping my hands tight together. I hoped she had too, that they hadn't found her, made her pay.

'I don't want Nan to know,' he insisted, nodding towards the corridor, where his grandmother was waiting. 'Thailand,' he said with a firm nod.

'The morning she left,' I said. 'Where do you think she went?'

'She'd gone by the time I was up. Walked down into the town and caught the first train out, I reckon. Get to Shrewsbury and there are connections for London or Manchester. Easy to disappear in a city, they say.'

'But not to Thailand. She had no passport, did she? And she couldn't have had much money.'

'She didn't take anything from us, if that's what you mean,' he said coldly.

'Did you ask at the station?'

'Not right away. I thought she'd come back, you see. Then, afterwards, well, no one could really remember. And I couldn't make too much of a fuss about it. That wouldn't have helped her, would it?'

'She wouldn't have gone to Lloyd, would she? Looking for work?'

He gave a bitter laugh.

'She had more sense than that. She knew his type.'

'But Willow went there.'

'Willow isn't as wise as she thinks,' he said.

'What was Willow doing there? You said she was waitressing?'

He nodded.

'She thought it would lead somewhere. The money was good. Lloyd can spin a yarn to them, silly girls. He has these parties. Him and his cronies. They drink, gamble, Lord knows what else. Willow wouldn't talk about it. Refused to admit I'd been right. But she wanted the money.'

She must have met Bryn there, I realised. She must know just what trouble he was in, and how much he was in debt.

'At least she won't be going back there now,' I said.

'No. I'm sure Lloyd will have already filled the vacancy,' he said bitterly. 'He's never short of candidates.'

I remembered the girl he'd bundled into the back of his Mercedes. What lies had Lloyd been spinning her?

'I feel sorry for Magda, putting up with all that, but she's trapped there, her and the baby. I just wish there was some way of getting her out.'

'She'll be out of there soon enough when Lloyd tires of her,' he said. 'Her and the kid. That's the time to pity her.'

He poured tea into Nan's cup. I shook my head when he reached the second mug.

'I must go. I've got an interview on the radio Tuesday to prepare for. Quilting and patchwork,' I added hastily, seeing his look of alarm. And, with luck, a long and delicious telephone call with Gabriel to look forward to when I got home. I hesitated, turned back to him. 'The photos of Seren the police took away. Have you any of them left?'

'Still a few up on the pinboard,' he said. 'Why?'

I shrugged. 'I didn't get a close look at them. I just wanted to know what she looked like.'

'Wait. I'll fetch one for you,' he said sullenly. He returned as I waited for him at the front door. 'There.'

I looked into the pale oval face, the bright mischievous eyes. She didn't really look like Willow at all, except for the shaggy mop of dyed red hair. But she did remind me of someone. A photo I had glimpsed on David Evans' desk.

'Thanks,' I said softly. 'Pretty girl.'

He took the picture back from me, held it close to him.

'She is. If I ever find the people who hurt her...' His eyes glittered with rage. 'How could they do that to a kid like her? Evil. Pure evil.'

I felt afraid of him again, yet I knew it was not me he meant to hurt. There was a rage inside him, yes, but that had more to do with his hatred of injustice. I wondered again what had caused him to quit his job and come back to The Garth. It was as if he were no stranger to bullying and intimidation. What had happened in his past to so embitter him? As I glanced at his taut frame, I saw that, with his Samurai topknot, there something of the warrior about him after all.

As I headed back through Llannon, I could not get the image of Seren out of my head. Peter's tale of her life was heartbreaking. No wonder she had been so careful to hide her tracks. She really didn't want to be found. But with no money, no friends, how had she managed to survive? By stealing again, selling her body? I felt sick and scared to think of her alone once more, without help. I knew a little of the helplessness and despair Peter felt.

It was after closing time at the museum. I turned into the main street and found my way down towards the riverside houses. Why did David Evans have that photograph of Seren? Was he a threat to her? What did he know about her past? I remembered the spark of interest in his eyes as I had talked about her. He knew more than he had told me, but what was he hiding?

'David? It's me, Bronwen,' I called out as he still had not answered the door. A light showed in the top-floor window. I could hear a thump of noise somewhere overhead. Was he working up in his studio? I knocked again, harder this time. 'David!'

I thought he had not heard me, or had chosen to ignore me, and was about to walk away when I heard the slow clump of footsteps down the stairs.

The door cracked open.

'You shouldn't have come,' he said hoarsely. He let the door swing open and I stepped inside. I stared at him in alarm. His face was blotched as if he had been crying. His shirt was half unbuttoned and awry, his neat waistcoat discarded.

'Whatever's happened?' I asked him.

He leaned forward and pushed the door closed. Slowly, painfully, like an old man, he climbed the staircase again, up to his study.

'I couldn't,' he said bleakly. He stepped aside and I saw the chaos of books and papers. It looked as if he had thrown everything onto the floor in a fit of rage. But it wasn't rage I saw when I looked back at him again. He gave a helpless shrug, his words slurring. 'It's worthless. All of it,' he said, kicking at the nearest pile. Then he dropped onto his knees, bending low over the scattered papers, and sobbed.

I crouched beside him, afraid for him. Whatever had made him throw away his life's work?

'David, you have to tell me. Tell me what's happened.'

I glanced hurriedly round. Where was the photograph? The picture of Seren? Then my gaze returned slowly, coldly, to him. 'What have you done?'

He pulled off his glasses, rubbed at his eyes.

'I never meant any harm,' he breathed. 'I never meant...' Again the sobs came, and he struggled to breathe. I waited till he calmed again. I took his hand and held it pressed between my own.

'Tell me what happened,' I said.

'She... she was working at the Daisy Chain. I'd get a coffee there sometimes. Or stop for a meal after work. She was sweet and kind. She... she took to coming into the museum. Asked me to explain the displays to her. She seemed really interested in finding out the history of the place. So I told her... I told her about my research. I know it was foolish of me. I think she was just lonely. But she was happy to listen. And I felt good. I felt I was doing something important. All this,' he said contemptuously, looking round him at the deluge of papers. 'She made me feel it meant something.' He gave a thin cynical laugh. 'She was like that. Kind. I asked her to come back, to see the work I was doing. She never seemed bored. I guessed she found life hard up at The Garth. But me, she had chosen me to be her companion, her confidante, you see.' He sighed, rubbed his eyes again, though the tears had subsided now. 'And then she began to tell me. About her past. Some of the things she had done. Why she had to run away. And it made me feel... Oh, I don't know. I loved her, you see. I fell in love with her. I never asked anything of her. I wouldn't. Not until she wanted... as if she would ever want me like that!' he said, snorting. 'Then she told me she had to go away. I tried to

171

dissuade her. I asked if she was happy up at The Garth. Lord, I even talked of buying a place for the two of us. Giving up my job so we could go somewhere we weren't known. But it wasn't what she wanted. I always knew that, I suppose. But it was hard to accept. I didn't want her to go. Just when I'd found her. It was like seeing all the light and warmth in my life snuffed out.'

'So why did she want to go? Did she tell you?' I prompted softly.

'Oh yes. It was Peter.'

'Peter?' My heart thumped in alarm. Surely I hadn't misjudged him?

'He wanted her to go back to college and sit her GCSEs,' he said. 'She'd missed out on so much. Had so little education. But that terrified her, going back to school. There'd be questions. She'd have to be registered, they'd ask her name. It would all come out. And she couldn't risk that. So one night, she came to me, she begged me to help her. What could I do? The last thing I wanted was for her to go, but they say, don't they, what you love most you must set free. I set her free.'

'What did you do?' I asked in growing alarm. He was calmer now, remembering her, relieved that he no longer had to hide his love for the girl.

'She told me to come and fetch her in the early hours, after Peter and Nan were asleep. I brought her back here. She'd been saving her money from waitressing and had some clothes hidden here. She told me to cut off her hair. Hacked it, more like, but she was adamant she had to change the way she looked. After that we dyed it black. Then she packed her rucksack and I drove her to Newtown and left her at the station there. I gave her money. Five hundred pounds. She didn't ask for it,' he added hastily. 'But I was afraid for

172

her. I told her to send me a postcard. Something, anything, so that I would know she was all right.'

'And did she?'

He bowed his head.

'No. I was just an embarrassing old fool. But as she walked away from me, she turned and came back. She kissed me. Just once. The only time. And then she was gone.' He put his head back, stared up at the beamed ceiling. 'Nothing I've done is of any consequence. Nothing of this matters,' he said bleakly. 'Just Seren. Just that moment, when we had our friendship, when I had the chance to help her. And now, because of me, the police think Peter Beddows killed her! I've been such a fool. A fool.'

I put my arm around his shoulder.

'You tried to do the best for her,' I said. 'You'd never have hurt her.'

'No! Lord, no,' he said aghast. 'I loved her, don't you see? She was the one good thing in my life. And now there is nothing.'

'It's not nothing,' I insisted. 'We just need to find Seren and make sure she's OK. And you have to tell the police.'

'How can I? You know what they'll say, what they'll think! How can I keep my job once this gets out? I'll have nothing left!'

'You have your integrity,' I said. 'You can't let Peter go on suffering. He's still under suspicion. Tell the police what happened.'

Love. David Evans had suffered for his infatuation with Seren, yet not once had he blamed her for leaving him. He had set her free. I wondered if I would be as strong where Gabriel was concerned. I didn't want to give him up. I wanted to fight to keep him. Yet I knew I had little to bring him back to me. Not while his daughter ruled his heart. I rang his number as soon as I got home. He should be back in London by now.

'Bron, I was just thinking about you.' His rich, deep voice purred down the phone to me, sending my stomach swirling. Even if it was a lie, I didn't care.

'I'm glad to hear it,' I told him. 'I just wanted to tell you that I love you. In case you forget.'

'How could I forget?' he said. 'Today was very special.'

My body tingled, remembering his touch, the feel of his skin against mine, the passion of his kisses.

'It's going to be a tough few months till I see you again,' I said, my throat husky with the threat of tears.

'You know what they say about absence,' he murmured. I did, but abstinence was more of a concern. Not for me. I was used to it, after all. But was Gabriel? I knew so little about him. Was he into self-denial? Could I really expect him to give up a lifestyle for me? I thought I was used to the single life by now. Suddenly I felt lonely.

'I wish you weren't so far away,' I said.

'It won't be for long, I promise. I'll be back in two or three months. Can you wait for me till then?'

He made it sound like a plea. Him, Gabriel Haywood, begging me to wait for him! As if I'd even look at another guy while there was a remote possibility of a relationship with him. He was all I wanted. And I wanted him now. And, incredibly, he seemed to want me.

'I guess I can try.'

15

SUNDAY

It was sheer bliss lying in bed with toasted teacakes and a pot of tea, and thumbing through a stack of quilting magazines. The wall hanging was finished and delivered, I had no workshops, no one to please but myself. I felt at peace. As long as I didn't think too much about Rachel's problems with Bryn, or worry over where Seren was. At least I was sure that David Evans would contact the police and admit his part in helping Seren to disappear, and that left Peter in the clear. The only thing that would have made the morning perfect was to share my bed with Gabriel. I rolled over, frowning. I wasn't sure yet how that was going to work out. Our lives ran on very different tracks. Even when he did come back in two months' time, would there be enough of an overlap to spend time together, to get to enjoy each other's company? He still had his work, based in London, always travelling.

Yet remembering his soft words sent a tingle through me. He loved me. He wanted to be with me. Nothing was going to change that. We both had enough determination and belief in one another to make our transatlantic relationship succeed, didn't we? I was just afraid that, as the distance grew between us, his need for me might fade.

With Gabriel still in my thoughts, I reached out to answer my phone and gave a lazily drawled 'Hi.'

'Bron?'

Rachel's anxious voice made me jolt awake.

'What is it? What's happened?'

'Lloyd,' she said, breathlessly. I could hear her footsteps ring out over paving. 'His henchmen came for Bryn this morning. They've got him up at the house.'

'Is he OK?'

'I don't know. Magda just called me. They're planning something. She said they were talking about the farm at Penwern. His aunt's place. I'm going over there now.'

'His aunt?'

I heard the slam of a car door then the engine start up.

'Can you come, Bron? I don't know what they're planning, but I'm scared.'

I was sitting upright on the bed now, my breakfast tray abandoned.

'Tell me where to come to.'

It was mid-morning when I started out from Ceri Cottage, but there was little light under the billowing black clouds. It felt more like evening. In sodden fields cattle huddled in the lee of the hedgerows. On the hills the scattered sheep turned their backs to the rain-laden winds. I flicked the windscreen wipers onto 'fast' as I drove through the puddles and mud, ascending the meandering lanes into the hills towards Penwern. Rachel had said the road was now open, the landslip cleared. I slowed as I turned into the lane, anxious in case the incessant rain had started another slide. At the side of the road I could see newly sawn logs piled, the remnants of the fallen tree. Wisps of police tape still clung to the hedgerows. Where were the bones now? Had the police any idea yet of who they belonged to?

At the next junction, I halted and checked the satnav on my phone. Another turning, a bridge across a stream that raced in torrents over tumbled boulders, then a steepening climb. Near the top of the slope was a wooden sign nailed to a gatepost. 'Penwern Farm'. The car rolled slowly forward, swinging round the bend, into a muddied cobbled yard. To one side stood a dilapidated stone barn, half the tiles missing from its roof. To the other stood a long low stone building with a sturdy chimney; part cottage, part cowshed, an old Welsh longhouse, its whitewashed walls almost hidden under moss and ivy. The tiny square of front garden was a mesh of ferns, brambles and thistle heads, and in the corner by the small window, the sturdy briars of a rose bush. A single mildewed bloom still clung to the topmost stem.

Rachel's Mini was parked at the gate. As I got out of the car, the front door opened.

'You came. I'm so glad,' she said. She stood on the doorstep, rain and tears on her pale bruised face. Then she hugged me. She felt cold, and was shivering. Her thin frame seemed more fragile than ever.

The small room was dark, the tiny square window almost hidden behind threadbare curtains. The centre of the room was filled with a solid square table, and a dresser stood against the wall, displaying a mismatched collection of flowery plates. A smoke-blackened inglenook fireplace housed a black iron grate with a bread oven. Beside it stood a wooden settle with faded cushions. Close beside the fire was an old wooden rocking chair where a figure sat motionless. As I drew closer to the fireplace, I saw the elderly woman hunched in a knitted shawl. Her skin was almost white and tightly drawn over the bones of her skull. How old was she? Nineties? She turned to watch me, her pale eyes surprisingly bright.

'Annie, this is Bronwen, the quilt lady I told you about,' Rachel said with an effort to sound cheerful.

177

'A visitor?' she said with a strong Welsh lilt to her words. 'Two in one day. Must be my birthday,' she said and gave a wheezy cackling laugh. 'Sit down, girl.'

I perched on the wooden settle opposite her. The room was cold, despite the logs burning in the grate. Did she feel the cold? Under the shawl she seemed to be wrapped in a patchwork blanket. Flannel, I recognised, stitched in a traditional pattern: red, grey, black.

'Rachel tells me you used to be a quilter, Miss Rees,' I said.

'Did she?' came the discouraging response. She turned her head to the fire. 'You'll take a cup of tea?'

'Thanks. That's kind of you,' I said. I wished I'd thought to bring biscuits at least, or a cake.

Rachel took the heavy kettle from the fireside and hung it from a hook over the fire.

'I'll go and fetch the cups,' she said.

'Let me give you a hand.' I followed her past the steep wooden staircase, ducking through the door into a tiny kitchen. There was a sink under the window, and a two-ring stove. No fridge or washing machine. Only a cupboard where tins and crockery were kept, and a larder for butter and meat. The ancient house was probably seventeenth-century, and little seemed to have changed in the intervening three hundred years.

'Where's Bryn?' I whispered. 'Have you heard from him?'

She shook her head.

'No use ringing from here,' she said. 'No mobile reception.'

'So what did Magda say about the farm?'

'She didn't hear the whole conversation. But I can guess. Annie never married. She farmed here on her

178

own after her brother died. She's got no family left except Bryn; her cousin was Bryn's great-grandma.'

'I still don't see why Lloyd's interested. I don't see him taking up farming.'

She gave an impatient sigh.

'When Annie goes, Bryn inherits the lot.' She saw my scathing glance. 'I know, I know. It's pretty run-down and the land's been sold off. It's probably not worth more than seventy grand. But she's lived like a hermit all these years. Bryn reckons she's got a fortune hidden some place. That's what he's banking on.'

'Her death?' I said, beginning to understand.

She nodded. 'Sooner or later he'll get the lot. Right now he could do with it sooner.'

'Couldn't he just ask her? I mean, maybe she'd lend him the money?'

'You see the way she lives. Of course she won't lend him the money! You think she approves of gambling, or drinking? They're deadly sins! She'd cut him out of her will if she found out.'

I sighed.

'We've got to do something. We have to protect her until we can sort Bryn out,' I said.

'Got any suggestions?' she snapped. It was a start. A moment ago she'd seem weak, defeated. Now I realised she hadn't given up entirely. There was still some fight in her. She wasn't alone any more.

I just had to figure out what we were going to do.

'Tea?' Rachel said, giving the pot a stir. There was no milk. We hadn't thought to bring any with us. She handed round the small fragile cups, spooned sugar into Annie's cup and stirred it for her.

'How do you manage on your own up here?' I asked the old lady.

179

'I get by,' she said sharply. 'The girl from Watkins' farm comes to see me a couple of days a week. Gets my pension for me, brings me my shopping.'

'Mrs Pryce?' Rachel said.

Annie nodded.

'It'll always be Watkins' farm,' Rachel explained. 'They were the family who lived there when Annie was a girl. The Pryces have farmed it for over thirty years.'

I smiled. I could guess Mrs Pryce was long past the 'girl' stage.

'Used to go there when I was a girl,' Annie said. 'I'd go with Mam. We'd all sit together and sew for a few hours and the women would gossip. Tea and slices of *bara brith* thick with butter. It was a real treat.'

'That's one of your quilts, is it?' I asked her, pointing to the flannel blanket over her lap.

'Years old,' she said proudly, 'but just as good as the day I made it. All sorts we made from scraps we found. Old petticoats, skirts, whatever we could get our hands on. People got to know. They'd bring pieces for us, down to the Watkins' farm. We'd make them up a quilt, just for a few shillings. When the war came, it was hard to get any spare fabric, but we managed as best we could. Make do and mend, they said. I could tell them a thing or two about that,' she said with a sniff.

'You've farmed here on your own for a long time, I hear.'

'There was a boy used to come. I had to let him go. Always complaining he was. When Pryce bought the Watkins' place, he wanted more land so I thought, why not? I'd worked as hard as any man since I was a young 'un. Pryce said it was time I took things easier.'

I nodded, though judging by the state of the cottage and her meagre lifestyle, there didn't seem to be much comfort. The flagstone floor was covered by worn rugs, and the only decoration was a dark framed picture of a Biblical scene of a shepherd and sheep.

Rachel tensed, her glance darting to the door.

'I... I thought I heard a motorbike,' she said. She relaxed then. 'No. Not coming this way.'

She hadn't told Annie that Bryn might come. We'd tackle that if and when he did arrive.

'It's getting dark. I'll make something to eat, shall I?'

'There's not much in. Shopping doesn't come till tomorrow.'

'That's OK,' Rachel told her. 'I've brought some eggs from home and a pack of bacon. Hungry, are you?'

Fried bread, eggs and bacon was as much as she could manage on the two-ring hob in the tiny lean-to kitchen. For once I didn't feel hungry. Ever since Rachel thought she had heard a motorbike, I could feel myself tensing at the slightest sound out of doors.

What if he didn't come? Rachel was intending to stay the night. I wasn't sure if I should leave her, but would there be room for me to stay in the cottage? I doubted it had more than one bedroom. I wondered if Gabriel had tried to ring me. Frustratingly, my phone showed no reception. How far would I have to go to get a signal?

After tea, we settled by the fireside together. Rachel kept watching the door, but no one came. I thought Annie was dozing, but when my eyes went to her again, I met her bright gaze.

'Where are you from, then?' she asked me.

I told her about my cottage, and about Ed.

'No children?'

181

'No. We didn't get chance,' I said. Well, Ed did. It was me he forgot about.

'I'd have liked children,' she said wistfully. 'Oh, Bryn's been a good boy to me. Comes to see me when he can. And Rachel of course. Time they were wed,' she confided, leaning across to me.

I gave a half-hearted smile.

'It would be nice to have grandchildren,' she said. 'Such a long time I've lived up here alone. It'll be good to think there'll be family to come after me. Someone to make the place a home again.'

'What was it like, growing up here?'

'When Mam was alive, it was joyous,' she said. 'She was always singing hymns. Life was hard then but she did her best for us. She loved us children. Then, when she died, everything changed.'

'How old were you?'

'Sixteen,' she said. 'They were hard times.' She leaned her head against the chair back. The rocker creaked slowly as she moved. 'Our father died soon after. It was left to me and Dafydd to carry on. Dafydd was nineteen. It was a lot on his shoulders, taking care of the farm and of me. It was the hardest time of all,' she said, with a shake of her head.

Rachel was on her feet then.

'It's Bryn,' she said. 'He's just come into the yard.'

She went to the door, and I could see she had half a mind to bar it shut. But then we heard his urgent steps, and his fist banged at the door and he lifted the latch.

He looked from Rachel to me, uncertain.

'What's going on here?' he demanded.

'Bron's come to ask your auntie about her quilts,' Rachel said quickly.

'Quilts, is it?' He looked me up and down in mistrust. I saw the tension in his face. 'There's no time for that now. Auntie, it's Bryn. You all right?' he said, pushing past us, his boots clattering over the flagstones. He knelt before his aunt and took her hand. I saw the inky patterns on his large fists. 'I need your help. You always said there was something for me, didn't you? But it's now I need it. You've got money hidden away, haven't you?'

'Money?' The old lady's eyes narrowed as she studied him. 'And what are you wanting my money for?'

'It's urgent. I wouldn't ask unless I needed it now. You know that.'

'Bryn, leave her alone,' Rachel said, going to him.

He stood up and pushed her away.

'Don't you understand? I need that money now! I can't wait until she's cold!'

'Bryn!'

'She doesn't need it!' he retorted. 'Look at this place! Years she's lived like this. And all the while the money's sitting there useless. Well, now I've got a use for it.'

'It's not yours!' she retorted.

'It will be soon enough,' he said coldly. He turned back to Annie. 'You remember where it is, don't you? In a cupboard? Buried in the garden? Come on, Annie,' he said leaning down to her. With his hands on the arms of the rocking chair he jerked it so she tipped suddenly backwards.

'There is no money!' she hissed.

'Course there is! You sold the land, remember? You've lived like a hermit all these years and not spent a penny. Of course there's money!'

'It's gone,' she said fiercely. 'All of it.'

'No,' he said, shaking his head doggedly from side to side. 'No. It's here somewhere. Rachel, start looking, will you? Now!' he ordered, his eyes blazing.

'Leave her alone!' I snapped.

'You don't get it, do you? That girl's awake. Willow. She's remembered what happened on the road. She knows it was me!'

'You? You ran down Willow?' Rachel gasped. 'Oh, Bryn, but how could you? You could have killed her!'

'Just find that money. I've got to get away from here before the police come. They were at the house. I saw them as I was coming home. I turned around before they saw me, but they'll be out searching. I've got to get away.'

'But it was an accident,' I insisted. 'Tell them what happened.'

'You think they'll believe me? After they hear what that girl tells them?'

Rachel stood before him.

'What did you do, Bryn? Tell me the truth.'

'The money!' he said fiercely, pushing past her. 'I've got to find that money. You ask her. I'll start searching.'

He opened the dresser drawers and cupboard doors, checked the kitchen cupboards, the larder shelves, then ran up the stairs. We could hear his footsteps thump overhead, then he returned and ran out into the garden. We heard the doors of the empty byre clatter open.

'Will he find anything?' Rachel whispered to the old lady.

Annie sat tight-lipped. She did not answer. She stared agonised into the fire as if she saw fiends there, dancing. She was scared, really scared.

'Make her some tea. I'll go and speak to Bryn,' I said. I ran out into the rain after him. He was halfway across the farmyard, heading for the derelict barn.

'This is stupid. She said there's no money. Why can't you just go to the police and tell the truth about the accident?'

He spun round at me, wild-eyed.

'Don't get it, do you? She was running away from me. I drove after her. I hit her!'

'What happened?'

'Lloyd's party!' he retorted. 'They were all tanked up after the game. One of them had lost more than he'd bargained for. There was a fight started. Willow got scared and took off. Lloyd's men were trying to stop the fight, so Lloyd tells me to go after her and stop her. I had no choice! I did as he said. Went after her. Near killed her. It's finished me,' he said bitterly. 'Finished, for good.'

'You owe him a lot?'

'Sold my soul, more like,' he said. 'I saw her in the headlights. She was running. Only suddenly she stops, and she turns to look at me. Only the car's still moving. Slipping. The road was all mud, see. And I hit her. She fell under the car. I thought I'd killed her. I couldn't think what to do. I just drove. Stupid, stupid,' he said, his face in his hands. His shoulders heaved. I thought he was crying.

'And Lloyd knows?'

'Of course he knows. I owe him. Thousands. There's stuff he wants me to do. Finish what I started. I can't,' he said, pleading. 'All I could think of was Annie's place. It might be enough to buy him off.'

'Except it isn't yours to give,' I said coldly.

'Not yet,' he said, glancing back towards the cottage. 'But there is money here somewhere, I know it. Yes,'

185

he said, frowning, 'I remember my dad saying. Years ago, they were building the lean-to for her. An inside loo and washroom. They had to dig out a hole for the septic tank. She had a right go at them. Didn't want to let them in with the mini-digger. Not at any price. Almost came to blows, they did. That's where it is. I knew it! She's buried the money, crafty old witch.'

He started running, in through the gate.

'Where's a shovel? You got a shovel, Annie?' he shouted, catching hold of her by her shoulders.

As I reached the cottage door, I saw the old lady slump back in her chair, her face drained white.

'You killed her! You bloody killed her!' Rachel screamed at him.

'No,' he said. 'No, she's breathing. Look.' He bent over her, frowning. Listening to her shallow, ragged breath.

'Get out!' Rachel snapped. 'You've done enough.'

He backed away from them towards me. I stood aside and let him pass. Presently I heard the motorcycle engine start up.

I let out a breath.

'He's gone,' I said. 'How is she?'

Rachel was holding Annie's hand, feeling for her pulse.

'OK, I think. It's her heart, I bet. My dad was the same. We should get an ambulance.'

'I'll try and get a mobile signal. Stay here with her.'

'I'll go. I know the nearest spot to get reception. I'll be ten minutes at most.'

The door closed.

'Annie? How do you feel now? Are you OK?' I whispered, close to her. She felt icy cold. I pulled the blanket closer round her. 'Bryn's gone now. You're safe.'

186

Her eyes flickered open and she studied me for a while, frowning, uncertain who I was.

'Sarah?' she whispered.

'It's Bronwen,' I said. 'Rachel's friend.'

'Where's the boy?'

'Gone,' I told her. 'We're getting an ambulance for you. How are you feeling?'

'Did he find it?'

'No,' I said.

She gave a thin smile and closed her eyes wearily.

'It wasn't really his fault,' she said.

I had other ideas.

'Dafydd,' she went on. I realised then she meant her brother. 'He never came to Chapel again after our parents died,' she said. Her eyes closed. She seemed to sleep again. I waited beside her, listening for Rachel to come back, for the sound of the ambulance siren. 'Nothing I did was ever right. He expected me to help round the farm. I was strong, but I couldn't keep up with him.'

'Just the two of you to run the farm, it must have been hard for you.'

'Sarah was the only joy in my life. She was my best friend,' she said, smiling. The rocking chair squeaked gently in time to her words. 'And her brother, Elis. He'd walk back with me along the river, to keep me safe. He wanted to marry me, you know. But I knew Dafydd wouldn't allow it. Sarah knew. She said we must make a quilt for our marriage bed. Elis drew a design for us to quilt, roses and leaves in a heart shape. Beautiful, it was.'

I sat upright, realising I had seen a design just like that. It was Nan Beddows' half-quilt. Her brother had been killed in the war. I had seen the initial 'E' embroidered on the quilt. Had he been Annie's sweetheart?

'I've seen another quilt like that,' I told her. 'At least, it's half a quilt. I wondered if I'd ever find the other half.'

'It's a long time ago,' she answered.

'Do you still have your quilt?'

'Oh yes,' she whispered. 'Upstairs. You may look if you like,' she said wearily. 'I'd like to see it again. It's time I did.'

Uncertainly I got to my feet. There was still no sound of Rachel returning. I didn't want to leave Annie, but it would take no more than a couple of minutes to run up the stairs and fetch the quilt.

Upstairs there was just one room with a tiny window set into the thick wall. Stout wooden beams shaped the walls and arched to form the eaves of the roof. A dusty curtain was draped on a pole across the room. Once it must have once divided the bedroom into two. There were two narrow iron-framed beds for brother and sister. A china jug and basin stood on a washstand by the staircase. I opened the door of the roughly made wooden wardrobe but inside were only some old clothes, a pair of worn leather boots, and a long black coat. There was a small chest under the window. I heaved up the lid. Inside I saw the folded fabric. I felt a jolt of recognition, an eerie feeling, of the past looming suddenly into the present like a tall black shadow. It was the missing half-quilt. The quilt I had seen at The Garth.

I lifted out the quilt carefully, turning it over to see the tiny stitches of the quilt pattern: a heart of intertwining roses and leaves in each corner, and the embroidered initials 'E' and 'A' in the centre of the hearts. Was Elis Nan Beddows' brother?

I hurried back downstairs.

'It's here,' I said. Annie smiled and held out her arms for the quilt as if to take a baby. Gently she spread it across her lap, her gnarled fingers stroking the fabric.

'I finished the quilt top that summer,' she said. 'Then we chalked the quilting pattern Elis had drawn. We stitched hearts into the four corners of the quilt, and more roses all around the border. You've never seen a prettier quilt. It was like a breath of summer. But I didn't dare to add our initials.'

'But you did add them later,' I said. I could see the elegantly scrolled 'E' in one corner, just as it was on Nan Beddows' quilt.

'Much later,' she sighed. 'After he'd gone.'

16

ANGHARAD

It was a good summer. Dafydd worked late into the evenings, scything and turning the hay. The days were long and there was much to do, and I knew he was pleased that the harvest was good. So I told Elis to come home with me and speak to my brother after Chapel on Sunday, when the hay had been carted and was safe in the barn. Only when Sunday came, and I took up my prayer book ready to go out, Elis's drawing slipped out of the book and Dafydd saw it. He saw the initials, and the heart Elis had drawn.

'What's this?' he said. I could tell he'd guessed right away. And I saw the fire in his eyes and I was afraid of him. I told him that Elis wanted to come and ask for my hand in marriage. My brother called me wicked names, and said I wasn't to see Elis again. He said a great many things best forgotten. He said I was betraying him, for if I left, he'd be alone with no woman to take care of him. And there was nothing I could say, for it was true. If I went with Elis as his wife, who would look after Dafydd and get his supper for him at the day's end?

Yet I loved Elis, he was the light in my life, and I wanted to be his wife. Perhaps I looked too stubbornly at Dafydd then. Perhaps I should have kept my head bowed. I don't know. For all at once I saw the flames in his eyes, and the Devil was in him. He struck me across the face, and his fists were hard from his work, and he had such strength in him, it was more than I could stand. I lost two teeth then, and my face was bruised, and I knew I couldn't go down to the Chapel. He took the drawing and threw it into the fire, then he barred the door and sat at the fireside till it was dark. If Elis came to the farm, I never heard him. Dafydd would not have let him in.

But Elis did not come. All week I was alone at the farm and Dafydd was out working dawn till dusk, and said nothing to me, except to take his meal with a grunt, and go off to his bed.

On market day. Dafydd went off in the cart as usual. He made me promise I would not go out. I would not go down to Watkins' farm. I was too scared of him to disobey. Besides, I was ashamed of the bruises and the mess of my mouth. How could I want anyone to see me, least of all dear Elis. He could not love me now. I wished I would never see any of them again. It would be easier that way, with nothing for Dafydd to reproach me with. But Sarah came. I knew she would. Dear Sarah came to find me. She thought I might be ill, she said. But when she saw my poor face, still bruised where Dafydd had hit me, tears came to her eyes, and she sat with me and put her arms around me and hugged me as if she was my mother and not my friend.

I cried for a long time then, for I knew that Elis would not come now and ask Dafydd for my hand. His meekness was no match for Dafydd's tempers. I did not want him to be hurt as Dafydd hurt me. I could bear anything for myself, but Elis must be spared. He had too much goodness in him to suffer as I had.

Dafydd was back early from market that day. I could smell the drink on him. He came in, already in a rage, and asked if I'd been out. I told him truthfully I had been at home all day, and then he saw the sewing basket, and he guessed that Sarah had been there with me. I swore I hadn't seen Elis, which was true, and by the time he had finished beating me, he believed I spoke the truth.

I went alone to Chapel on the Sunday. I knew Dafydd would be watching me, and I dared not walk with Sarah, nor look in Elis's direction. I knew Sarah would have told them about the bruises that even now could be seen on my face, and the gap where my teeth had been. They could not see the bruises on my body, for Dafydd was more careful now. I saw the way Elis looked about him, searching for Dafydd. When our eyes met in Chapel, I gave a shake of my head to warn him he must say or do nothing. Then, on the Friday, when Dafydd was gone to market, Sarah came again and she brought our marriage quilt, for it was finished now. I had never seen such fine stitching for the quilting. It was so beautiful, it made my heart ache, for I knew it could never be our marriage quilt. Dafydd would never allow it. I told Sarah I couldn't keep it. She said she just wanted me to see it, to see how beautiful it was with Elis's pattern. And she'd stitched his initial into the corner.

'But it won't be needed,' I told her. 'Not by me. You must keep it for your own wedding.'

She said I must not give up. I must be patient. I asked her how Elis was. She said he was fretting. She said 'He talks of leaving. Of taking you with him, and going away to find work. He can't bear to be apart from you like this.' But I told her I could not leave my brother.

'One day you must,' she said. 'Dafydd will have a wife of his own.'

'Only if he finds one in the alehouses of Llannon,' I told her, for he would meet no one else, since he never came to Chapel.

She shook her head and refused to give up hope.

'Just be patient,' she said.

And so I waited. And Dafydd came home earlier from market, and smiled and was courteous to Sarah as she took her leave of us. He would have walked her home down the valley, but she said there was no need. I wondered if she was afraid of him then. And I saw the hunger in his stare and realised he wanted Sarah for his wife. While the idea of having Sarah close pleased me more than anything, I could not wish her the kind of life I had with Dafydd.

I didn't go back to the Watkins' farm for a while, for fear of upsetting Dafydd, and I avoided Elis at Chapel. But then I couldn't wait any more and when Dafydd set off for market I went down to the farm. I wanted to tell Sarah we must make a marriage quilt of her own. She'd no sweetheart then, but I thought it wouldn't be long till she found someone and would be betrothed. Such a pretty thing she was, and always dimples in her cheeks when she smiled. I remember Elis catching sight of me as I came along the path by the river, and he waved to greet me. There was such delight in his face. I felt sorry then for having avoided him so long. He left his work, and came and sat with us in the parlour, and I knew he still felt the same about me, and that he would be patient too, and wait for the right time to ask Dafydd. I let Elis walk back with me along the river, and he handed me from boulder to boulder where the little streams ran down to join the river and the ground was mossy and tufted with marsh grass. And then there was the steep climb up the hill to the farm, and he held tight to my hand all the way, and when we reached the farm gate he stopped and put his hands around my waist, and kissed me. And I knew I was ready to be his wife, and that I would wait no longer.

'I'll come on Sunday after Chapel and ask your brother if I can marry you,' he said to me.

I was scared at what Dafydd would say, but my heart was singing at the thought that Elis and I would soon be wed. And then I saw Dafydd come out of the barn, and I knew he had seen us together at the gate.

I told him we were to be wed, but he didn't answer. Instead he drew off his thick belt and thrashed it against me. And when I fell down, he kicked me with his heavy boots. I cried out but he didn't heed me. All I could see was the Devil burning in his eyes, and his foul words cursing me. And when I next woke, it was morning. It pained me to move but I got up from the floor and set about my tasks, raking the ashes, setting the fire. There wasn't a sound from the house or barn. I didn't know where Dafydd was. I guessed he had gone out into the fields to his work. It was as much as I could do to get the cows in from the field to milk. I could barely lift the pail for the pain it sent through me. Each breath cut like a knife. Then at nightfall he came back. He did not look at me, but sat at the table and spooned in the stew I set out for him, made with the dumplings that were his favourite. After that, still without a word, he went out, a wire loop he used for catching rabbits hanging from his pocket.

Dafydd was away from the house at first light and didn't return till dark. I knew then he was waiting for Elis. I thought of running down the valley to the Watkins' farm to warn Elis not to come, but still I was suffering from the beating, and I was afraid Dafydd would see me. So I waited, in pain as much for wishing Elis would stay away as with the ache in my bones. I was about to creep upstairs to my bed when I heard Dafydd's boots on the cobbles of the yard, and I saw him lead out our pony and begin to pull on the harness.

194

I asked him where he was going, but he didn't answer. He just went on fastening the buckles of the harness, backing the pony between the shafts of the cart.

I begged him, 'Tell me where are you going!'

He glared at me then, and I saw the Devil come in his eyes again.

'Hold your tongue!' he said. 'You'll learn obedience yet, my girl!'

I felt sick and scared then, afraid of his rage, but I was even more afraid for poor Elis, so I ran out to him as he stepped up in the cart, and I asked him.

'Where's Elis?'

He yelled at me to hold my tongue. I saw then, in what light there was from the cottage window, a dark staining on his waistcoat. It looked like blood. I stepped back, my head spinning.

'What have you done?' I asked him. I felt more fearful than I'd ever been in any of his rages.

'He's gone,' he said, and his face took on a smile of such wickedness, it made my blood run cold. 'He won't be coming to paw at you again,' he said. 'He's run away, like the coward he is. He won't be coming back.' With that, he cracked the reins and drove the cart out of the yard.

Sarah came that afternoon. She was in a wild state, her pretty hair awry and mud on her skirt. She must have come running up from the farm, taking the path along the river. She asked me if I'd seen Elis. Her eyes were wide and fearful. 'He didn't come home last night,' she said. She told me her brothers had been out searching but there was no sign of him. Then as she touched my arm, I flinched away with the pain of Dafydd's beating. She knew he had hit me again and she told me I must not stay here. 'Come back with me,' she begged. But I told her I could not. I could not leave Dafydd. And then he came. He must have been watching the house. He knew they would come here to look for Elis.

'What's this?' he asked, as if he didn't know.

'It's Elis,' I told him, and looked him in the eye. 'He's not come home.' I felt strangely calm then. As if there were no more he could do to me. He had destroyed me and I no longer feared him. Then he turned to Sarah and told her, as he'd told me.

'He was here,' he said. 'He came to ask for my sister's hand in marriage. I told him I'd never see her married to a *twpsyn* like him. He went off whimpering about his heart being broken. Said he'd go away and find work, and prove that he could keep her. I suggest you look in Llannon for him, for last I saw him, he was headed that way.' Then he invited her in. Said she should take a sup of tea to calm her, for she looked in some distress. And all the while he was smiling, and I didn't trust him.

'No, thank you,' she answered him. Her glance went up to him, wondering if she could believe him, and I thought she didn't trust him either. She said she had to get back, for her parents would be waiting, and she asked me to go with her a little of the way.

Dafydd said I'd work to do in the house. 'But I can walk with you, and keep you safe,' he said, all smiles.

'There's no need,' she told him, but he held out his hand to her.

'Come along,' he said, all hearty. 'You and I have some talking to do. I'll walk with you.'

So with a backward glance at me, she let him take her arm and lead her back down the path. My stomach churned with panic. I did not trust him. I did not trust that docile smile. It was a long enough walk along the riverside, and few about to hear her if she cried for help.

'Let me walk with you,' I said, for I couldn't bear to see her go along with him so docilely. But Dafydd cast me such a glare, I stepped back from her.

'Your place is here,' he said, and he came back up the path, and with a thrust of his hand, pushed me back inside the house. I fell backwards, and hit my head against the stone floor. I felt sick and giddy, and when I tried to stand, my legs would barely support me. But I had to get up. I knew that. So I got to the gate, but there was no sign of Dafydd or my Sarah in the yard. Then I heard a loud, terrified scream. It came from the barn. I ran, though I could hardly get a breath, and there I saw them, in the barn, in the piled hay. Dafydd had Sarah pinned beneath him, her legs kicking and her skirts flapping up around his naked backside, his breeches pulled to his ankles.

'You're mine now!' he was yelling at her, all the while she sobbed. 'There's no denying me now!'

And I took up what was nearest, and with that strange cold courage I had felt before, I hit him hard across his head. I felt the blood spurt hot on my face. And he let out a single cry like the beast he was, and the hump of his body relaxed and slipped to one side.

I saw Sarah, ashen-faced. She was struggling to push away the weight of him. I pulled him from her, and took her in my arms and hugged her as once she had hugged me.

'There now, you're all right,' I told her. 'He can't hurt you now.' For I knew he was dead. I'd seen Dafydd dispatch pigs and sheep enough to know when the light of life was gone from them.

For a long while we sat there in the hay together, but I knew we had work to do. I saw the silent heap of a body.

'You must help me now,' I told her.

She looked with round, scared eyes at his lifeless face.

'I cannot touch him,' she said.

'Then you must help me dig,' I told her.

Under the cottage window there was a patch of newly dug earth where I had planted a briar rose. With fork and spade we made the hole deeper, longer. I took the wheelbarrow over to the barn and hauled and heaved until I had the weight of him tipped into the barrow, then, with many a stop for breath and strength, I pushed the barrow across the yard and up the garden path.

When it was all done, Sarah asked me, 'What will you do now?'

I told her, 'We will say he has gone away. He went with Elis, to make his fortune.' That summer they were saying there'd be a war soon. If it came, we'd say they'd enlisted as soldiers. After that, it would be easier.

'But if Elis come back?' she said. And I did not answer.

When we had washed the blood and the mud from our hands and clothes, I took out the wedding quilt and cut it in two.

'One half will be big enough for my single bed,' I told her. 'You must keep the other half. It will remind us of Elis and what happened, and we will never tell a soul. It will be our secret.'

'But your brother,' she whispered fearfully.

'We'll say that Dafydd went away. He went with Elis to make his fortune.'

She looked so frightened, her hands, her body shaking. 'They'll never believe us. They'll know what we did,' she whispered.

'No.'

I got up and went to the dresser. I found a sheet of paper and my pen and ink. Dafydd had never had much of a hand for writing. It wasn't hard to write a letter such as he might have done.

'Dear Sister, forgive me. I am gone after Elis. We will get a boat and go to America. We will work and when I have money enough, we will send for you to come. Your loving Brother.'

'There,' I said, blotting the page and wiping the nib. 'It is done. And no one will question us.'

I walked back with her then, along the river. When we came to the place where the river widened into a shallow pool, I made her sink down into the water, then I pulled her out.

'We'll say you fell in and almost drowned,' I told her, 'and that's why you are so distressed. Tell them about the letter. I will keep it here so they may see it, but I doubt they will ever ask.'

17

BRONWEN

We both heard it at the same time, a distant siren. A few minutes later the ambulance rolled into the yard, lights blazing, flashing round the old stone walls.

Rachel bent down to Annie and gently roused her.

'They're here now. They've come to make sure you're all right.'

'I'm fine,' Annie said, stirring. 'All this fuss and bother... waste of time.'

She peered up as two green-uniformed paramedics came into the room.

'Hello, Miss Rees. How are you feeling now?' the young woman asked, a bright smile on her face. She knelt beside her on the cold stone floor.

Rachel and I waited anxiously while Annie's pulse and heart rate were checked. They filled in a lengthy form, peered at the print-out from the monitor.

'Has your doctor prescribed any medication for your heart?' the young woman asked.

'Nothing wrong with my heart except old age,' she said.

'You need something to keep the rhythm steady. We'll take you back with us and they'll have you sorted out in no time.'

'I can't leave my home,' she said appalled.

'I can stay with her,' Rachel said. 'I'll have the doctor come and check on her tomorrow.'

There was a debate between the two paramedics, and hurried conversations on their radio. The young woman returned, her smile undimmed.

'I think it will be better if we take you back with us,' she said. 'Can you get some things together for her?' she asked Rachel.

'I can't go. I can't leave here,' Annie protested.

'It'll be all right. It won't be for long,' I reassured her, hoping it was true. 'They'll sort your heartbeat out, and you'll feel much better. It's just a matter of finding the right pills for you.'

'Come with me,' she said, grabbing my hand. 'I don't want to go on my own.'

'Of course. Look, I'll bring the quilt too, if you like. You can tell me a bit more about it on the way.'

Rachel had gathered up a few things in a bag and followed the ambulance in her car as we set off across country to the hospital in Newtown. It was strange to think Willow was there too. When I had a chance, I wanted to see her and find out how she was. Had she remembered what had happened at Lloyd's place? Did she know it was Bryn's car that had hit her?

In the ambulance, I sat holding Annie's hand. She looked small and scared, strapped into the narrow bed. I tucked the quilt over her.

I was aware of the jolting of the ambulance over the ruts in the road. Then there were streetlights. I guessed we were driving through Llannon. It would be another twenty minutes till we reached Newtown. Annie closed her eyes. Perhaps her shock at Bryn's violence had started to abate.

'What have you done? What have you done?' she murmured in some distress. Was she dreaming? Or was it Bryn she was thinking about?

The paramedic checked her pulse again.

'Try and rest. We'll soon be there,' she said gently, but Annie only moved her head weakly from side to side on the pillow.

201

Annie's eyes opened. She turned to find me. I felt her fingers tighten on my hand.

'It was our secret,' she said fiercely. 'Sarah kept her half of the quilt to remind her. I kept mine. Elis never came back to the farm.' She gave a sigh. 'I think she always knew. But now they've found his body, up in the woods. She came to see me that night. She'd heard about it on the radio. She had to know, you see.'

'Nan Beddows?' I said.

She nodded.

'He killed him,' she said softly. 'Dafydd killed him.'

The ambulance was slowing. We had turned in at the hospital, and were pulling up outside the Emergency unit.

'He had the Devil in his eyes that day,' she said. 'He couldn't bear for me to be happy. He would not let me marry Elis. So he went after him. And then he thought he could have Sarah. I saw them. In the barn,' she said fiercely. 'I saw what he did to her. He forced her. My sweet Sarah.' Tears came to her eyes.

She glanced towards the opening doors, to the tall figure of the paramedic who was stepping up into the ambulance to fetch her, and she fell silent, her lips tightly compressed. I squeezed her hand and tucked the quilt around her as they lowered the trolley to the tarmac.

I looked round for Rachel. It was visiting time now, and the car park was full. It would be difficult finding a parking space. I hoped she was all right. She had looked so shocked at the way Bryn had behaved, and at his revelation that he had almost killed Willow. How could she ever come to terms with that?

They wheeled Annie into an empty room in the Emergency unit. A nurse came and hooked her up to a heart monitor.

'The doctor will be along shortly to see you,' she assured us. I sat down beside the bed, Annie's hand clutching mine. She was dozing now, but still she held me. It seemed she needed someone to cling to, after living alone for so long. Her words troubled me. The rape she had witnessed. Her own brother. And what had really happened to Nan Beddows' brother, Annie's sweetheart? Nan told me her brother had been killed in the war, but Annie had been sure her brother had killed him. His body had just been found in the landslip.

'He was a brute and a bully. I could not let him go unpunished.'

Her soft voice startled me. I thought she was sleeping, but as I turned to her I saw she was awake, her eyes glistening.

'God will judge me,' she said with defiance.

'What did you do?' I whispered.

'I hit him. He never stirred again. Sarah helped me bury him. She found someone to love her. I knew she would, though it was ten years till she married. I never saw her after that. I could never marry. I could never leave the farm.' She turned her face away from me and hummed softly. I recognised the old hymn tune: '*Cwm Rhondda*'. 'The roses always grew well there under the window,' she said softly.

I stared at her, appalled, trying to make sense of what she had told me. All these years, alone at the farm, with her dead brother buried in the garden. Her burden. Her guilt. How had she lived with that? For love, I thought then. Because she had loved Sarah more than any man. She had lived to protect her.

Rachel peered round the door at us.

'How is she?' she asked.

I looked at Annie, dozing now. A new ease had come into her face since she had last spoken. She had made her confession. 'She's peaceful now,' I said.

Rachel didn't look any more at ease.

'I saw Bryn's motorbike in the car park,' she said. 'What the hell's he doing here?'

It was as well it wasn't me linked to the heart monitor. I felt a sudden panic drum in my chest. Willow was here, wasn't she? The girl he had almost killed. And her memory was beginning to come back.

With a chilling clarity I remembered Bryn's words as we'd stood in the farmyard.

Lloyd had told him to finish what he'd started. Did that mean he'd tried to kill Willow before? That hitting her with the car had not been an accident?

'What is it?' Rachel asked urgently, seeing the panic in my face.

'Willow. The girl Bryn ran down. She's here. Something happened that night at Lloyd's. Something he doesn't want her to remember.'

Lloyd was using Bryn to shut her up, and Bryn had little choice but obey him. He was deep in debt to him. Had sold his soul.

'Stay with Annie, would you?' I asked her. 'I just need to check…'

I left the Emergency unit, following the signs for the main wards. The corridors were busy at that time of the evening, with families meeting up, taking patients down to the café and shop. As I passed the League of Friends' café, I caught a glimpse of a familiar figure in the queue at the counter. Bright lipstick, painted fingernails. She was clutching a pack of cigarettes. I stopped. It was Willow's mother.

'You're Imogen's mother,' I said, recalling the girl's name.

She looked sharply at me.

'I remember you,' she said, almost in accusation.

'Library service,' I said brightly. 'How is your daughter?'

'Making a good recovery, they say,' she said. She looked weary suddenly, the steely surface cracking a little. I almost felt sorry for her. 'She's coming home with me very soon.'

'That's good news. Is she still on the same ward? I'd like to pop in to say hello,' I said. 'To see if she enjoyed the books I left her.'

'Ward 203, second floor,' she told me. 'But she's sleeping. That's why I thought I'd take a break. Dying for a shot of caffeine and a ciggie,' she said with the ghost of a smile.

'I won't be long,' I promised.

I hurried along the corridor, weaving between the ambling groups, the wheelchairs. There was already a little cluster of people waiting for the lifts. The lights showed third and fourth floors. My heartbeat was racing with anxiety. Just where was Bryn? Why had he come if not to do Lloyd's bidding?

I pushed through the swing doors and started up the stairs. By the time I made the second floor I could hardly breathe. This was no good. I really had to get fitter, lose weight. I paused for a moment, gulping air, then emerged into the main corridor.

Ward 203 led off to the right, past a row of doors. The ward was divided into small bays, six beds to a bay, and every bed seemed to have several visitors grouped around it. There was no one at the nurses' station. I couldn't remember which room Willow had been in before. I looked round for help and saw a nursing assistant pushing a trolley with urns and cups.

'I'm looking for Willow, Imogen,' I corrected. 'She's in a side room.'

'Go on down the ward, second door on the left. I think the doctor's with her, though.'

'Thanks.'

I found the door with Imogen's name in felt pen on the white sign beside it. The curtain was drawn across the window. I wondered if I should wait. I couldn't hear voices from inside the room. Then there came a sudden scuffle of noise. I took a breath, and pushed the door open.

The man in the white coat was bending over her. She seemed to be writhing on the bed. It was a matter of seconds as I stood there, but then I recognised the tattoos on his outstretched arms, and as I moved forward, saw he was holding a pillow over her face.

'Get off her!' I yelled out, and launched myself at him.

Bryn spun round, his face crimson with fury. As I reached him he swung his fist towards me. Somehow I ducked but, caught off balance, I stumbled and fell to the floor. In seconds he dropped onto me, his fingers digging into my neck, pressing, squeezing, as he tried to strangle me, thudding my head against the floor.

Choking, desperately gasping for air, I felt the room swirl about me, black, sparking with stars. And above me, his face, his eyes bulging, fired with the flames of Hell, the Devil within him.

'Willow?'

She was my first thought when the air came rushing back into my lungs. I coughed, tried to sit up. The weight had gone from my chest. What had happened?

I focused slowly on the shoes, the legs, then up to the faces ringed around me, the young doctor in green scrubs bending over me.

'She's all right,' she said.

'I'm so sorry, Bron.' Rachel dropped to her knees beside me, her face white, eyes tear-filled. 'He almost killed her. You too.'

'Lloyd,' I got out, my voice hoarse. My throat and neck were sore. 'He sent Bryn. Pay off his debts.'

She nodded in understanding.

'He won't get away with it,' she said vehemently.

'Where...?' I tried to look round, but everyone was more concerned with keeping me still, it seemed, which did not reassure me at all.

'The security guys have got him,' she said. 'The police are on their way.'

'Willow?' They helped me to my feet, steadying me for a moment. I looked past them and saw Willow lying propped up on her pillows. She managed a half-smile.

'OK. I'm OK,' she whispered. I reached out and touched her arm.

'Lloyd sent him. To shut you up. He was afraid of what you'd remember.'

She nodded. 'I remember Bryn's car. I thought he'd kill me then. But he swerved away. I think he lost his nerve.'

'What made you run from Lloyd's?'

'There was a fight. Too much drink, and someone didn't take kindly to losing all his money,' she said. 'Mervyn and Gareth were busy trying to stop the fight, so I ran to fetch Lloyd. I heard the music. I know he gets strippers in for his special guests. But it wasn't that. I went in to tell him and that's when I saw... They were watching a video. I just felt sick. I turned and ran. Lloyd must have sent Bryn after me.'

'You told the police?'

She gave a shake of her head.

'Only just remembered. Thanks to Bryn,' she said, and gave a weak, tearful smile.

We waited in a small overheated office near the hospital reception. After checking me over, Dr Elliott decided she wouldn't need to keep me in overnight, and, thankfully, Annie was doing well and would probably be discharged the following day.

As the police constable took a brief statement from me, I wondered what Bryn would tell them. Would he tell them that Lloyd had instructed him to run her down deliberately? What would the police reaction be to Willow's statement? I didn't want to try and imagine the kind of video they had been watching. And, with Willow's background of abuse, I wasn't surprised it had so alarmed her.

It was midnight by the time we made it back to Penwern for me to pick up my car.

'Why don't you stay? You look all in,' Rachel said. 'I'll sleep in Annie's bed. I'd made up the spare bed for me, but you can take it.'

I had to admit I didn't feel much like a drive back across country to Bishop's Castle.

'If you're sure you don't mind,' I said.

'You're kidding. I owe you,' she insisted. 'Let me at least have a chance to repay you.'

I followed her up the narrow staircase and flopped exhausted onto the bed.

18

MONDAY

I woke, stiff and sore, with the light streaming through the thin curtains at the window. Rachel was rummaging in the cupboard. She let out an exclamation.

'How come he missed this?' she said.

I sat up to see what she had found. She was holding a tin box. It was a Carr's biscuit tin, painted like a sampler with a crinolined lady on it, and a motto in cross-stitch, '*little said is soonest mended*'.

'It was in the bottom of the wardrobe,' she said. 'Under the lisle stockings. I was trying to find some clean clothes to take for Annie. They should be discharging her today.' She gave the tin a shake. It rattled.

She sat on the bed beside me and prised off the lid. Inside was an assortment of coins: large copper pennies and halfpennies, a few farthings and threepenny bits, and several brown ten shilling notes. With them was a crumpled fragile piece of paper: a letter in faded, scrawled ink. It was signed '*Your Brother*'. I peered at the jagged letters. I could just make out the words.

'*I am gone after Elis. We will get a boat and go to America. We will work and when I have money enough, we will send for you to come*'

I frowned. Had Annie told me the truth? Was her brother's body really buried under the roses?

'This must be Annie's hoard,' Rachel said with a rueful smile as she counted out the coins in the box. 'She said she'd got enough saved to bury her. I'll have to take her into the bank with me and see if they can change the old money for her.'

209

'Bet those notes will fetch more than face value on eBay,' I said, trying to smile. I felt only a great weight of sadness, that this was the sum total of Annie's life. She had lived with her guilt for so long.

'Not a fortune, is it?' she said wryly.

'Hard-earned, for all that.'

'My grandparents were the same. It meant a lot to them to know they'd have a good send-off. Never wanted to be a burden to anyone.' She tucked the tin back under the stockings in the wardrobe and closed the door. 'Makes me so furious to think Bryn would have taken it, every penny she'd saved all her life, just to pay for his own stupidity. He doesn't deserve it. And now, Lloyd's as good as made a murderer of him. He'd have killed Willow to save his own worthless neck! I could kill him myself.'

'At least they'll have charged him and locked him up. You don't have to worry about him coming back.'

'No. No, I suppose,' she sighed. She stared at the little window, her fists bunched, as if determined not to cry. 'I tried to make a go of it. It wasn't perfect. Not by a long way. But we could have made it. If he hadn't been such a bloody fool.'

'It wasn't your fault. You'll get over this, and move on,' I said, dimly aware that I was sounding a little like Willow.

'I just feel so guilty, about letting him cause havoc. I should have known. I should have stopped him.'

'There was nothing you could have done,' I said. 'You were here for Annie when she needed you.'

She went downstairs and returned with a jug of warm water and stood it on the washstand. I splashed my face quickly and dressed, trying to shake off the anguish I still felt at Annie's confession. By the time I went downstairs, I could smell toast.

'Hope you like scrambled eggs,' she said, standing aproned in the kitchen doorway. 'That's all there is.'

She'd already got the fire going, though the room was slow to warm. At the window, the rose briars tap-tapped at the glass as the wind caught them. Annie had told me she had buried her brother there. He'd lain there for over seventy years. Good roses, she had said. I shuddered. No wonder she had never dared to leave. She had to stand guard over her secret. Their secret, I thought, for it was Sarah Watkins who had helped Annie bury him. Or Nan Beddows, as she was now. She would know the truth about the letter. The truth about Dafydd's death. I knew I could never ask her. The two women had lived apart ever since, united by that dreadful memory, by two halves of the wedding quilt.

'You OK?' Rachel asked, setting the plate of toast and eggs in front of me.

I nodded. 'Just thinking. Must have been a lonely life up here for her all these years.'

'It was what she wanted, I suppose.'

Was it just the secret that had bound her there alone, unable to share her life with anyone else for fear they might discover her guilt? It was sad and cruel to think how her brother's death had continued to dominate her life. But I suppose her faith and her sense of justice would have accepted her fate. She had taken a life, after all, and for that, her own life was forfeit, just as if she had been imprisoned. And she had done it for love. She had no regrets.

'I'll go back to the hospital this morning and see how Annie is,' Rachel said. 'She'll be glad to get home. It must all be bewildering for her.'

'You'll ring me and let me know how she is?'

'Of course.'

'Will you be able to stay here with her?'

211

'For a while,' she said. 'I can't go back to Bryn's place. We'll need to decide what's best for Annie, and what she wants to do now. Perhaps she can be persuaded to go into a residential home. Somewhere she'll have people to take care of her.'

'Perhaps,' I said, but doubted it. I didn't think Annie would ever leave Penwern Farm.

I left the farm after breakfast, hoping to make it back to Bishop's Castle in time to change and get back to Llannon library for my afternoon workshop. I still had hopes of using Annie's quilt in the exhibition, though with an edited version of its history. On my way down the hill to the road, I decided to call in at Watkins' Farm. They would need to know what had happened to their neighbour.

The farmhouse was a sturdy whitewashed building with a cluster of well-kept outbuildings. I turned in at the gate and drove into the yard. A woman appeared at the back door, a reassuringly plump figure in a baggy plaid shirt over her T-shirt, and faded jeans.

'Mrs Pryce? I'm Bronwen Jones. I've just been visiting up at Penwern Farm. I'm afraid Annie was taken ill yesterday. She's OK, but they took her into Newtown hospital, just to be sure.'

'I thought I heard an ambulance go by. I never guessed,' she said. 'Is it serious then?'

'An erratic heartbeat, I think. They're giving her some medication.'

'She's a fighter,' she said. 'Stubborn as they come. You've got to admire her, though.' She smiled then. 'Good job you were there. I was just about to make a coffee if you'd like one?'

I glanced at my watch. Maybe fifteen minutes wouldn't make too much difference. I could still make it back to Llannon by two. And I was eager to find out more about Annie's life up at Penwern.

'Thanks, that'd be great,' I said.

The elderly black-and-white sheepdog lying stretched out in front of the Aga barely raised its head as I walked into the kitchen, but its feathery tail wagged against the slate-tiled floor.

'She's lived there all her life, I gather.'

'And she won't think of moving out,' she said. 'I know. I've tried to persuade her. She won't even come down here for a meal now and again.'

'She said you keep an eye on her, and fetch her shopping.'

She shrugged. 'It's the least I can do. How's she going to cope when she comes home, though?'

'Rachel will be staying with her for a few days,' I said. 'Her...' I stopped. I'd been about to call Rachel her granddaughter but of course she wasn't. It was just that Annie seemed to regard her as such. I wondered how I would face the situation at Annie's age. I had no children either. No one to look out for me. 'She's the girlfriend of Annie's great-nephew.'

She nodded. 'I've met her. Nice girl. Bryn not around then?' she enquired.

'No,' I said. 'And he may not be for a while.'

'No?'

I sipped my coffee and didn't risk explaining. I couldn't be sure yet what was happening with Bryn. I could sense her studying me, her gaze coming to rest on the reddened skin on my neck and throat.

'Of course, things may well change now,' I said. Now that Elis's body had been found, I thought. 'Rachel will need to sort out Annie's finances. We're not sure if she has money hidden away somewhere.

Apparently she sold the land to you when you came here.'

'It wasn't quite like that,' she said. 'My husband knows more about it than me, but her farm and land were leased from the Watkins. Old man Watkins was fond of Annie. She was like a daughter to him. When he died, he left the house to her rent-free for her lifetime. He wanted her to know she'd got a roof over her head for as long as she wanted it.'

'Then there is no money?'

She gave a shake of her head.

'Not from the farm, no. We've put a bit away every year to maintain the house, but frankly she's not the easiest to help. She took some persuading to have the bathroom built. There used to be an earth closet out the back before that. Then when we turned up with the digger to put in the septic tank, she tried to stop us. Said she didn't want her land digging up.'

'I can imagine she was anxious about anything new and unfamiliar,' I said evenly, remembering the briar rose.

'Anyway, it's a listed building now. Not many traditional Welsh longhouses left untouched. It'll be impossible to modernise the house even if we tried, and I'm not sure we'd want to. But we've always thought of that money as Annie's fund. If she needs money now for her care, she's welcome to it. Brian keeps the books so he can tell you how much it all adds up to, but it's a few thousand.'

A few thousand. Safe from Bryn. That was good news.

Kate was waiting anxiously as I made it to the library for the afternoon workshop.

'I didn't think you'd come. I heard about the goings-on at the hospital. How are you?' she asked, inspecting the marks on my throat.

'Fine,' I said. All the same, I didn't feel quite so perky when I saw the little crowd gathered to join in my quilting session. It seemed I had become a celebrity. I recounted the events at Willow's bedside all over again. I desperately wanted to creep away to somewhere quiet and sleep.

As I left the library after the workshop, I saw Peter coming out of the Daisy Chain café. He waved when he caught sight of me.

'How are you? I heard what happened at the hospital.'

I smiled. It seemed everyone in Llannon knew what had happened.

'You've been to see Willow?'

He nodded. 'You saved her life.'

'How's she coping?'

'She's a bit shaken. She was doing so well up until then. They're hoping to discharge her tomorrow. She's decided to go back to live with her mother for the time being.' He gave a rueful smile. 'Her decision. But at least she's going back to college in September. She wants to study law, she says. So she can go after the villains.'

'You'll miss her.'

'We'll keep in touch. I'm getting a mobile phone. She knows I'm here for her, any time she wants me. Besides, never know when I might need a good lawyer,' he said and smiled. I thought he looked much calmer now. I could see something of the easy-going, peaceful man he must have been before Willow's accident. It wasn't any penance for him to be living and working up at The Garth, I realised. He did it because he loved it. I was glad for him. Glad he had been able to choose a way of life that had meaning for him. Even if it meant Nan Beddows would have to wait a while yet for him to find a soulmate.

'There'll be a court case, though. It won't be easy for her, reliving it all,' I said. 'She'll be glad of your support.'

'It'll be tough,' he agreed. 'But not as tough as Lloyd's going to find it.' He gave a wide satisfied grin. 'He's had it coming to him for some time. The police arrested him early this morning.'

'So he used Bryn to try and shut Willow up. Only Bryn couldn't go through with it. At least, not the first time. Second time round he made a better job of it,' I said ruefully, my hands going to my throat as I remembered.

'I hope they put them away for a good long while.' His eyes sparkled. 'And that's not the only good news. They found Seren.'

'They did? Where is she?'

'Liverpool. She was caught shoplifting. The police took her in and did a check on her fingerprints. A match came up with the ones from The Garth. DS Flint turned up yesterday with the photo they'd sent through. Asked me if I recognised her. It's been two years, mind, so she does look different. A lot thinner for a start, and her hair's short and now she's blonde. But it was Seren all right.'

'They've arrested her?'

He shook his head. 'Someone must have told Flint about her. Told him about her past life, the hell she was running from. He made some enquiries. They've struck a deal. The shop's not pressing charges. The police want her as a witness for a case they've been building.

216

She's going into their witness protection programme. New identity. New name. She'll just disappear again, but they'll be there to keep an eye on her.'

I glanced down the road towards the museum. I was glad I had been right about David Evans. He had had the courage to tell them about his involvement with the girl. Now they knew what she'd been through, about the men who had used her, given her drugs. The fear she had lived with, that she would never be free of them, that they would come after her to silence her.

'Flint wouldn't give me any more details, but she'll have a new life waiting for her once the trial is over. She can go to Thailand, if she wants to.'

'And how is Nan?' I asked him. 'It must have been a shock to her finding out it was her brother's body they found in the landslip.'

'It's not been easy. Brought back too many memories, I think. But at least she knows where he is now,' he said. 'It's what they call "closure". All these years she's lived not knowing where he is, what happened to him. After I took her to see Annie, she was very low. Perhaps she always knew he was dead, but until his body was found there was always that slim hope that he'd gone away and made a new life for himself.'

'It is Elis then?'

'I told Flint about Nan's brother disappearing all those years ago. We won't know for certain till they do some DNA tests to see if there's a match, but in Nan's mind there's no doubt.'

I nodded. I had much the same impression from Annie. She was certain it was Elis, that her brother had killed him.

'She wants me to arrange a proper funeral for him at the Chapel once the body's been released to us. That's

217

what I'm here for,' he said with a glance back into the café. I could see Rhiannon watching us from behind the counter. She raised her hand to wave. 'Rhiannon's going to do the catering for us. A proper funeral tea, up at The Garth.'

Closure. I suppose it was for Nan Beddows. Had she really helped to bury Annie's brother at Penwern Farm? Or should I believe the letter, that Dafydd had gone away to America to seek his fortune? No wonder her memories were making her uneasy. I wondered how Annie was coping. Should I ring DS Flint and ask for his help? But what would that achieve? There'd be more questions, formalities. I had the distinct impression Flint was a man to go by the book. No, perhaps there were some secrets better left buried, for the time being at least. Of course, it all depended on what would happen to Annie. If she went into a nursing home, she would have no choice about what happened at the farm. Perhaps it was better to have a quiet, informal word with DS Flint. I tried his number when I got back to my car. Thankfully it went to voicemail. I left a message.

19

TUESDAY

The phone call from Rachel woke me at eight.

'It's Annie,' she said. 'She didn't make it. I stayed with her at the hospital. She just drifted away. Early hours of the morning.'

'I'm so sorry,' I said, but perhaps, now she had made her confession to me, she felt she no longer had to keep tight hold of that thread. She was free at last. 'How are you?'

'Oh, OK. Bit down, I suppose. I'll go on over to the farm later and start sorting out. I don't think there'll be a lot to do, but there's no one else to do it. Not with Bryn gone.'

'If you want a hand,' I offered.

'It's OK. I'll ring Watkins Farm. I'm sure Mrs Pryce will help. Oh, and I've been thinking, about that quilt of Annie's you liked. I think she'd want you to have it.'

'You sure? It's quite an heirloom.'

'I'd be happier knowing it was safe with you,' she said.

'So where will you go now?'

'There's a flat over the Daisy Chain. Rhiannon said I can use it for now, till I get sorted. It'll be handy for the market. I've asked Peter to help me build a website. I need an online shop if I'm ever going to make enough money to live on. Actually, it's quite exciting, isn't it?'

'It's great news,' I said.

'I just wish I still had Magda to make her beads for me. They were gorgeous.'

Magda. Of course. She was free now, wasn't she? Lloyd was out of her life.

'Have you spoken to her?'

219

'Briefly. She rang to tell me they'd arrested Lloyd. She wants to get away from here, as far as she can. Can't blame her, can you? At least Lloyd won't be troubling her for a good ten or twelve years. Conspiracy to murder, illegal gambling, possession of indecent images, and whatever else they find when they turn over that particular nasty little stone. By then she'll have made a new life for herself and her son.'

'It's his son too,' I reminded her.

I heard her chuckle.

'Not if he gets a DNA test done.'

'You mean…?'

'It isn't his son. It's Mervyn's. Big ol' bear of a man that he is, but underneath he's quite a softie. He's had a thing for Magda from the start. He looked out for her. She's really very fond of him. Not enough to want to share her life with him, but the boy, well he could do worse than have Mervyn take him out to play footie now and again.'

'Mervyn,' I repeated. And into my mind came an image of the big man crouched in front of a pushchair, of a large index finger gently touching the child's cheek. 'Of course.'

'Lloyd never twigged,' she said. 'When he does, she'll be far enough away for him not to do anything about it.'

I made the radio station with ten minutes to spare. Through the soundproof glass I could see Evan's lean figure hunched at the console, his thin face looking insect-like under the outsize headphones. His voice chirped over the speakers as he gave the weather update and traffic news. He caught sight of me and waved. His smile broadened as he introduced the next track.

'And now, for our next guest, a golden oldie. From the sixties, it's The Searchers and "*Needles and Pins*".'

Was he implying I was a golden oldie too? He grinned, and I forgave him.

A young woman in a skimpy skirt and black leggings ushered me into the studio, settling me down in front of the microphone as the track played.

'Switch your mobile off,' she whispered.

'OK?' Evan asked me. 'I thought we'd start with you telling us a bit about your quilts.'

'Great,' I said. 'Though I'm not sure how well that's going to look on radio.'

'We'll do a phone-in after we've chatted. Stir up a bit of interest in that exhibition of yours.'

'That'd be brilliant.'

The track faded out.

'And now our next guest, our very own Quilter in Residence, Bronwen Jones. Welcome, Bron. Now, you're here to tell us about some of the gorgeous quilts you're going to be showing. What's the title of the exhibition?'

I smiled back at him.

'Every quilt tells a story,' I said, and not all of them were happy ones, I thought.

After the broadcast I went back to my car. It had stopped raining. That was a plus. As I clambered into the Land Rover, I switched on my phone. Moments later it rang. I recognised DS Flint's number. My stomach lurched. So what should I tell him? That there was probably a body buried at Penwern Farm, a murderer and rapist killed by his sister, aided and abetted by his victim? Who was that going to help? I wasn't even sure that Dafydd deserved a decent burial.

Annie said he'd been a brute and a bully. She'd been ready to face her ultimate judgement, unafraid.

'Miss Jones, I got your message. How can I be of help?' he asked, ever cool and efficient.

I hesitated. No, I couldn't tell him about Dafydd.

'I just wondered... about the body in the landslip. Nan Beddows is convinced it's her brother. He went missing years ago.'

'I've been in touch with Mrs Beddows and her grandson,' he said, noncommittally. 'We'll need to do some tests.'

'If it is Elis, I think it will almost be a relief to her, after all these years not knowing what had happened to him,' I said. And finding a body up at Penwern farm would not be, I decided. 'It must have been awful for her.'

'A murder victim too. Not that we'll ever know now who killed him,' he said.

'No. I don't suppose so,' I said. Once the DNA results were through, and the body was identified, he could close the case. Move on. I swallowed. Hang up, I thought, my fingers clenched around the phone. Hang up before you say something stupid.

One day someone would want to refurbish the farm. When the bones were found, there'd be an inquest, of course, but it was all so long ago. There was nothing to connect the body with Nan Beddows. Nothing but a quilt cut in two, and that, I'd decided, would not be going on display. I didn't want any awkward questions.

'Thanks,' I said, realising he was waiting for me to say something. 'I'm glad you found Seren. Peter Beddows told me. She'll have a new life at last.'

He grunted. 'It won't be a picnic, a court case like that, but I've spoken to her. She's prepared to give it a go. She's a fighter.'

'She deserves a chance,' I said. 'Oh, and I hear you've arrested Lloyd.'

'We did, but he's out on bail.'

'Lloyd? But how could you? He tried to have Willow killed!'

I heard him sigh.

'We didn't have much choice,' he said. 'People like him can afford the best lawyers.'

The passenger door opened. I gave a gasp as I recognised the man who got into the passenger seat. It was one of Lloyd's burly henchmen.

'Drive, Miss Jones' he grunted. 'Lloyd wants a word with you.'

'What? But where is he?'

'Just drive. I'll tell you where to turn off. And don't do anything stupid, will you?' he added with a thin smile.

I slid the phone to the floor of the car and started the engine, my heart pounding.

'What does Lloyd want with me?' I demanded.

'A talk,' he said. 'He's very upset. You brought the police to his house, Miss Jones. He doesn't take kindly to that.'

'I'll bet,' I said under my breath. I drove.

As we cleared the town and took the lanes he pointed out, I could see a car following close behind me: a black BMW. I didn't recognise the driver, but from the shape of him, his bald head, the dark suit, I guessed it was another of Lloyd's team.

'So where are we going?'

'Shut up and drive,' he snarled. 'Here. Turn here.'

The narrow road climbed the hillside, winding its way towards the summit. We rumbled over a cattle grid, onto open moorland. Sheep scattered from the verge at our approach. To my left the hillside fell away steeply. I slowed at each bend, taking my time.

'Pull off here,' he said. There was a picnic sign. I turned the car. A short drive brought us up off the road onto a patch of level ground that gave a view across the hills and valleys. There were picnic tables across the close-cropped grass. At any other time the view would have been breathtaking, but I'd just seen Lloyd waiting in his Mercedes, and I felt sick.

I watched in the mirror as he emerged from his car, wrapped his long camel coat about himself, and approached. My passenger slid from his seat to make way for him.

'I enjoyed your radio interview, Miss Jones,' Lloyd said, easing himself into the seat beside me. 'Good to know exactly where you were when I wanted you.' He gave a thin-lipped smile, his cold blue eyes gleaming.

'What do you want?' I said, still clutching the steering wheel, my hands shaking.

He reached across and took the keys from the ignition, jingling them between his fingers.

'A few loose ends to tidy up,' he said mildly. 'Like you and Willow.'

'Willow?' I stared at him. I knew she would be one of the main witnesses against him. 'Where is she?'

'She's being taken good care of,' he said, nodding slowly. 'Very understanding woman, her mother. She told me a great deal about Willow. I don't think I need worry too much what the girl will say in court. After all, she's hardly a reliable witness, is she? She has a history of invention and hysteria.'

I glared at him. 'You'd bring that up in court? That her mother's boyfriend abused her?'

He spread his hands. 'What else can I do? It's her word against mine. The police won't find any evidence

224

of porno videos. Not at my home or at any of my clubs. All legal and above board. And as for thinking I had anything to do with sending Bryn to kill her, it's just a nonsense. No,' he continued, 'don't get me wrong. I feel sorry for the kid. Why put herself through the hassle? I wouldn't be surprised if she decided she couldn't face a court case after all.'

'You tried to have her killed and you think you can get away with it?'

'As I said, she is in a very precarious mental state. Prone to fantasy. Whatever happened between her and Bryn isn't my concern. How could it be? I'm sure her mother will help her see the truth.'

I pictured the woman in high heels and bright lipstick. Had she sold out to Lloyd? I wouldn't be surprised.

'It's been a busy morning,' he said. 'So much to tidy up.'

I shot him a sharp glare. What was he up to? Was Magda safe? Had he decided to silence her, too?

'Where's Magda?' I asked him.

'Ah. Magda,' he said calmly. 'Yes, we had a little chat. Seems she's decided she wants to go back to work after all. A friend of mine's got a club up in Liverpool. He's looking for hard-working girls like Magda. He'll make sure she's fully employed,' he said with a leer. 'Turns out she wasn't the motherly type after all.'

I felt sick with fear. What had he done? I doubted Magda had gone willingly. Not without her child.

'The baby,' I said. 'Where's the baby?'

He frowned slightly, and he gave a slight sigh of annoyance.

'It was my mistake. Too soft-hearted, you see, that was my problem. I should have had him tested before. The police finding those bones, now that made me think. I had a DNA test done. Turns out the child isn't mine at all. Fancy that!' he said with mock surprise.

'Where is he?'

He glanced at his watch.

'Right now, in the arms of his new family, I should think. Got a good price for him, too.' He grinned as he saw the appalled look on my face. 'You'd be surprised how many people there are out there, desperate for a child. And what they're prepared to pay. I'd no idea. Mervyn's taken him this morning to exchange for a pramload of money.'

'Mervyn?'

I stared at him, and couldn't help the laughter that bubbled up inside me. It was such sweet relief, even in the midst of my fear of Lloyd and what he could do, to realise Mervyn had his child. He wouldn't give him up. Had he got Magda too? They'd done it. They'd escaped. I couldn't stop laughing.

His hand slapped me hard.

'Shut up!' Then his phone rang. I saw from the expression on his face it was not good news, at least not to him. Someone sounded very angry.

'There must be some mistake. Give me five minutes,' he snapped. He got out of the car and punched a number into his phone. I guessed there was no answer from Mervyn. Lloyd glared at me. He beckoned his men, and got back into the car.

'I've been patient long enough,' he said. 'I told you before I didn't want you interfering in my business. But you would insist.'

'How can I possibly harm you?' I demanded, hearing the tremor of fear in my voice. He heard it too and gave a thin smile.

'You won't,' he said. 'I'll make sure of that.'

'But there's nothing I can tell the police,' I protested.

'That's what I want to be sure of,' he said. 'You're the only one who saw us together. The only witness. I didn't know she was under age. She was keen enough. And now she's heard I was arrested, she knows I've got money, greedy little cow thinks she can blackmail me. Only it's her word against mine.'

I stared at him, trying to make sense of what he said. What girl? And then I remembered. The young waitress from the launch evening. I'd seen him with her, her skirt bunched up to her waist, I saw him bundle her into the back of his car. Had she been as willing as he pretended?

'You... you raped her!' I said furiously.

'Nonsense. I never touched her. I had to leave the party early on business. I never saw her leave the building. No witnesses,' he said breezily. He held out his gloved hand. One of the men handed him a bottle. It was a bottle of vodka. He unscrewed the top and handed the bottle to me.

'Drink,' he said. 'Call it a celebration. A good send-off.'

'I don't drink vodka,' I insisted.

'Today you will,' he said. 'In fact you'll drink quite a bit of it. And when you drive off, your car won't make it at the next tight bend. Quite a steep slope, down through the trees. It may be some time till they find your body, but you won't suffer. You'll be dead long before then,' he told me. 'A tragic accident. Sad, lonely and unloved. You can understand it, can't you?'

And I did understand it. Where was Gabriel now? If I really meant so much to him, could he have flown off to be with Lydia, and left me? A promise to come back in two, maybe three months' time: what kind of commitment was that? I was deluding myself, because I

227

couldn't face the truth. Gabriel had taken what he wanted and now he had gone.

'The police will find a pile of empty vodka bottles at your cottage,' Lloyd informed me. 'Now, drink!'

He pushed the bottle to my lips. I struggled against him in fury at the way he had treated Magda, Willow and the waitress. He couldn't get away with it. I took a gulp of vodka and spat it full in his face. He glared at me, wiping his face, then got out of the car and handed the bottle to one of the men standing guard.

'Finish it,' he snarled.

The two men climbed into the car, one either side of me. One grabbed my hair, pulling my head back, the other gripped my chin and forced my mouth open, pushing the bottle against my gritted teeth. He pinched my nose closed. I fought, desperate to breathe. My mouth opened. I swallowed, half choking. The liquid burned down my throat, my stomach churning as the alcohol hit. I wanted to be sick.

'Hold her down!' Lloyd shouted.

Their grip tightened. I tried to buck, to kick against them, but they were strong, determined. The vodka splashed over my face, down my neck, into my mouth. I spluttered, coughing, but had to swallow. Seconds later I heard Lloyd shout.

'Get out!'

The men stopped suddenly, released me. They were out of the car, running. I heard the bottle smash to the ground. The engines started up. Then I heard it. Police sirens. They were coming up the hill.

The Mercedes screeched down the bank onto the road. I saw the flash of lights as the police cars gave chase. One of them slewed in front of the BMW as it tried to turn out of the car park. Doors slammed. There were shouts, the sounds of a scuffle.

I staggered out of the Land Rover, my body shaking, with hardly strength enough to stand. Then I was violently sick on the tarmac. I sank to my knees, head bowed.

I hadn't heard the car roll quietly to a halt. Dimly I was aware of someone standing before me. Shiny black shoes, neatly pressed trousers, dark grey. My gaze rose unsteadily.

He crouched down, reached out a hand and laid it gently on my shoulder.

'Are you all right, Miss Jones?' DS Flint asked.

I wanted to answer, but my throat still burned. Tears flooded my eyes.

'My phone... you heard it all?' I got out between sobs.

'Most,' he said. 'Until we lost the damn signal coming up the hill.'

'Lloyd?' I whispered. 'You've got him?'

'He won't be troubling you again,' he said gently.

When I woke, the room was almost in darkness. Just a lamp shining somewhere nearby. But where was I? Where was my car? Lloyd, I thought in panic. He had kidnapped me. He was going to kill me.

I tried to sit up. My head thumped. I heard a movement. With an effort I focused and saw DS Flint coming towards me. I recognised my kitchen. My sofa. I frowned. How had I got here?

'How are you feeling now?' he asked, kneeling beside the sofa where I lay.

'Awful,' I said thickly.

'Your neighbour's just gone home to feed her dog,' he told me. 'She'll be back in a minute. She's going to stay the night with you.'

'Vi's here?'

He nodded.

'She let us in,' he said. 'I drove you back, since you were in no state. I thought you'd prefer that to hospital.'

'Thanks,' I said, groaning as I remembered the vodka.

'I had a long chat with Vi while you were sleeping.'

'You did?'

He nodded, a light dancing in his cool grey eyes. Whatever had Vi been telling him?

'You're quite a remarkable woman,' he said.

I gave a shake of my head. It made my skull pound. Not a good idea.

'I'm nothing special,' I said.

'She said you'd say that,' he said. He smiled then. I hadn't seen him smile before. The lines crinkled around his eyes. 'She's told me a lot about you.'

'Don't believe half she tells you,' I croaked.

'I'd rather make up my own mind,' he said. 'I wondered if you'd come and have dinner with me. When you're feeling better. Would you?' There was an unmistakable eagerness in his tone.

'Me?'

He nodded.

I looked up at him in some surprise, though the movement brought a stab of pain in my head. He was serious. He really wanted to take me out to dinner. I remembered what Lloyd had called me. Sad. Lonely. Unloved. That's the bit that had hurt the most. Unloved. And at the time, I had believed him. Gabriel had gone. He was on the other side of the Atlantic, back with his daughter and his ex-wife. There was no place for me in his life for now. Would there ever be?

The pulse of pain in my head calmed for a moment. I managed to look up at him again without wincing.

'Yes,' I said. 'I'd like that very much.'

FURTHER INFORMATION

The mid-Wales town of Llannon is my invention, although it was inspired by my visits to Llanidloes, once at the heart of the mid-Wales flannel industry. Llanidloes is home to the wonderful Minerva Art Centre, the base for the Quilt Association and its inspiring quilt exhibitions which feature quilts from their collection of mainly Welsh quilts as well as work from modern textile artists.

While the farms and cottages in the story are drawn from my imagination, I was inspired by the ancient Welsh longhouse at Gilfach which is owned by Radnorshire Wildlife Trust, though the residential part of the house is in private occupation. I have also invented a hospital in Newtown, for the sake of the story.

My thanks to Kim Bishop, my eagle-eyed proofreader, for her help with the text.

TEN TEMPLATES

The following motifs are drawn from the story and include Lady Godda and her sisters, simple tree and house shapes for a child's quilt, as well as the rose heart motif from Annie's quilt. The templates can be photocopied and resized for your own art projects. You can also download the templates as PDFs or as cutting files in Silhouette Studio and Craft Robo GSD software, from my website at:

www.beanpolebooks.co.uk/QD2_MfM_10motifs.html

These template designs are my copyright. Please do not copy and share or sell the templates without my written permission.

LINKED HEARTS

ROSEBUD

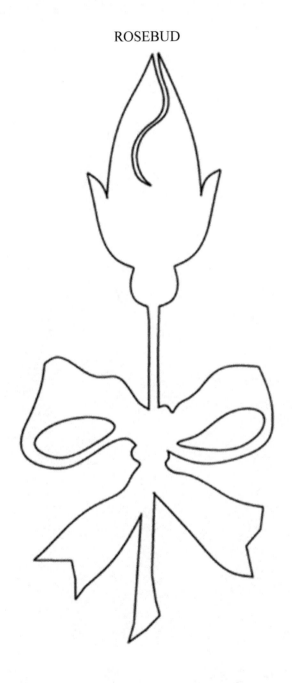

CELTIC KNOT

DAISY CHAIN

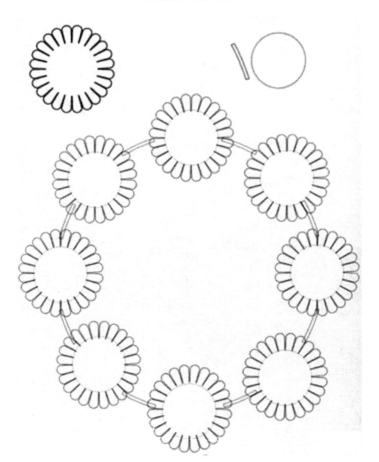

ROSE HEART

SIMPLE HOUSES

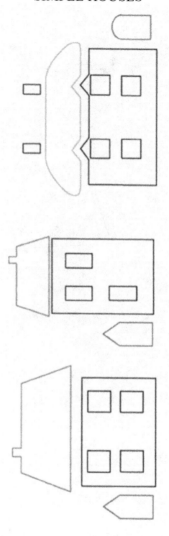

SIMPLE TREES

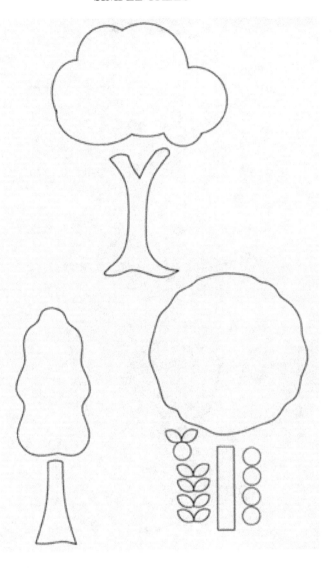

LADY GODDA AND HER SISTERS

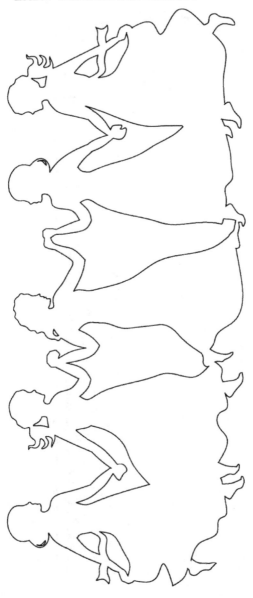

SHEPHERD BORDER

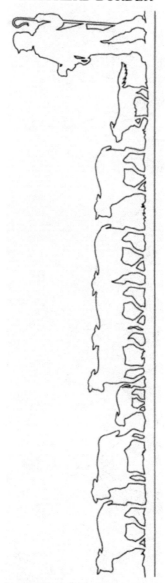

Also by Karen Lowe:

A PATCHWORK OF POISON
A mystery in forty motifs

Amazon Reviews

'Good well written story of interest to anyone into quilting. Moves well between past and present and very hard to put down.'

'I really enjoyed this book and was enthralled by the seamless ease with which the author worked the story of the past with that of the present.'

'This is a well-written cosy mystery which was a gripping read. It's full of twists and turns stereotypes on their head... The ending was unpredictable and surprising; I can really recommend this book.'

'This is a delightful story... Her writing is immediate and believable and we care about them both. I enjoyed this book very much.'

The antique quilt was exquisitely embroidered with flowers and leaves. A labour of love, Bronwen thought. Until she discovered a darker purpose to the quilt's design.

'A Patchwork of Poison' is the first story in the Quilt Detective series and introduces textile artist Bronwen Jones who is establishing a new career in South Shropshire after her divorce.

Sixteen-year old Cat asks Bronwen for help in uncovering the history of her heritage quilt, and the rumoured lost inheritance. But when Cat disappears and a schoolfriend is found murdered, Bron discovers the thread that links past and present, and the deadly secret the quilt conceals.

On sale at Amazon as a Kindle download
and from Kobo.com
Also available in paperback from Amazon

ISBN-13 978-0953177066

STAR GARDENS SERIES

DEATH IN THE PHYSIC GARDEN

Amazon reviews:

'well written with a complex plot and some interesting characters'

'I enjoyed this so much that I immediately bought the next in the series'

'Excellent writing. Good storytelling'

'This mystery features some beautiful description and heaps of gardening knowledge, as well as a gritty murder puzzle and a difficult, but promising relationship that begins to develop in this first book of what surely will be a series. For the discerning reader'

Readers reviews:

'the atmosphere and location are brilliantly done'

'marvellous flower detail'

'I never guessed the ending'

Death in the Physic Garden introduces garden designer Fern Green who has escaped from London and her abusive boyfriend to find refuge in the remote South Shropshire hills. Setting up her garden design business, Star Gardens, she believes she has found peace and safety at last until she discovers the body of her first client, wealthy herbalist Joshua Hamble, dead in his physic garden. As she becomes ensnared in the Hambles' family secrets, she unearths a trail of murder and revenge. As DI Drummond warns her, 'Gardening can be a dangerous business.'

Read an extract at www.beanpolebooks.co.uk

On sale at Amazon as a Kindle download
and from Kobo.com.
Also available in paperback from Amazon.co.uk

ISBN-13: 978-0953177042

DEATH IN THE WINTER GARDEN

2011 Quarter Finalist,
Amazon Breakthrough Novel Award

Amazon reviews
'This is so well-written!'
'I loved everything about this excerpt - from the setting (the damp, rainy countryside, and let's not forget the potentially beautiful gardens), to the sense of loss woven throughout the excerpt, and then to the characters...There is a wonderful sense of familiarity here as well, I instantly felt like I could know the characters, which made me invest in them right away. Excellent'
'If you like your crime novels cosy with an unusual background then I would recommend this book and its predecessor, Death in the Physic Garden'
'More gorgeous gardening from the talented and capable Fern Green. I fell in love with her in the previous book (Death in the Physic Garden), and this time around that love deepened. An enjoyable read'

'Death in the Winter Garden' continues Fern Green's career, and her relationship with hunky Welsh detective, DI Ross Drummond. When the body of a newborn baby is found in the long-neglected garden of Plas Graig, Fern discovers that the secrets of the past still haunt the living. When a girl is murdered in nearby woods, the echoes of past wrongs can no longer be stifled. But Fern soon discovers that there are some in the village who would prefer the past remained buried. As she tries to find a link with an apparent suicide six years before, her quest to unearth the truth puts her own life in danger.

On sale at Amazon as a Kindle download and from Kobo.com. Also available in paperback from Amazon.co.uk
ISBN-13: 978-0953177059

WITCHES & WARRIORS:
LEGENDS FROM
THE SHROPSHIRE MARCHES

Retold by Karen Lowe
Illustrated by Robin Lawrie
Published by Shropshire Books

'A very worthwhile book, guaranteed to win friends for this county'
The Junior Bookshelf

From Shropshire's rich folklore come these stories about the giants, knights, ghosts and witches who populate the landscape, teamed with wonderful illustrations by Robin Lawrie. Read about Jenny Greenteeth, Nicky Nicky Nye, and the escapades of Shropshire's own Robin Hood, Wild Humphrey Kynaston. Meet Ippikin the Robber Knight, if you dare, and be enchanted by the story of Wild Edric and his Elf Bride

Paperback on sale at Amazon.co.uk
or order online from
www.beanpolebooks.co.uk
where you can read an extract